CRYSTAL
CONNECTION

SCIENCE SQUAD
ADVENTURE SERIES
#2

CRYSTAL
CONNECTION

Tanya Lloyd Kyi

whitecap

Young scientists should check with an adult before starting any experiments in this book.

Edited by Carolyn Bateman
Proofread by Elizabeth Salomons
Cover design and interior illustrations by Jacqui Thomas
Cover photograph by getty images ™ creative
Interior design by Margaret Lee/bamboosilk.com
Interior layout by Henriett Kuti

Printed and bound in Canada

National Library of Canada Cataloguing in Publication Data

Kyi, Tanya Lloyd, 1973-
  The crystal connection / Tanya Lloyd Kyi ; Larissa Vingilis-Jaremko and Evelyn Vingilis, authors of non-fiction.

  (Science squad adventure series 2)
  Includes bibliographical references.
  ISBN 1-55285-511-2

  I. Vingilis, Evelyn. II. Vingilis-Jaremko, Larissa. III. Title. IV. Series.
PS8571.Y52C79 2003   jC813'.6   C2003-911064-8

The publisher acknowledges the support of the Canada Council for the Arts and the Cultural Services Branch of the Government of British Columbia for our publishing program. We acknowledge the financial support of the Government of Canada through the Book Publishing Industry Development Program for our publishing activities.

At Whitecap Books we are committed to protecting the environment and to the responsible use of natural resources. We are acting on this commitment by working with suppliers and printers to phase out our use of paper produced from ancient forests. This book is printed by Webcom on 100% recycled (40% post consumer) paper, processed chlorine free and printed with vegetable based inks. We are working with Markets Initiative (www.oldgrowthfree.com) on this project.

for Larissa

Contents

About the Canadian Association for Girls In Science

The Canadian Association for Girls In Science (CAGIS) is an association for girls by girls. The purpose of CAGIS is to promote, educate and support interest and confidence in science, technology, engineering and mathematics (STEM) among girls. CAGIS was started in 1992 by Larissa Vingilis-Jaremko at age nine, when she became concerned that many girls were becoming turned off science at an early age. Yet Vingilis-Jaremko realized that science literacy is critical for society's survival in the twenty-first century. She decided to start a science club to encourage girls' interest in STEM.

Where local CAGIS chapters exist, CAGIS members meet monthly during the school year. In a girls-only, social and supportive environment, CAGIS members explore STEM. Members have the opportunity to meet professional women who are working with STEM daily. Members are as likely to meet with a microbiologist and learn about the science of microbes as they are to meet with an artist and learn about the science of print-making. Plenty of time is spent doing hands-on activities. The ultimate goal is to help girls appreciate how STEM surrounds us and is used in everything, and how critical it is to our understanding of the world.

As part of the yearly membership, CAGIS members receive a quarterly newsletter, and a one-year subscription to *YES Mag*— Canada's science magazine for young people. CAGIS members also develop their writing and leadership skills by helping run CAGIS and by writing up their CAGIS events and other stories for the newsletters and the feature column in *YES Mag* called "What's Up at CAGIS?" CAGIS has an interactive website, where CAGIS members can connect with other members across Canada and the world. The website is especially important for members who do not live near a CAGIS chapter site. It has both a public site and a private site, which has a password secure "Clubhouse" for CAGIS members only so that they can safely and comfortably use the computer. The Clubhouse includes regularly changing features of Professor Hootie's Did You Know? column, great Canadians in science, Science Squad Webisodes, STEM games, STEM activities and experiments, and a message board where members can share ideas, jokes, stories, find science penpals, and more.

Since CAGIS's inception in 1992, CAGIS has had over 3000 members across Canada and internationally. Surveys conducted by CAGIS have found a positive impact on members' knowledge of STEM and on school science. To learn more about CAGIS check: **www.cagis.ca**

1

Ferry Tale

"What?" Sue yelled, looking back at Nicole and Gina. She could hear their voices, but the wind was whipping their words away. The three girls were standing on the deck of a ferry, their hair snapping behind them and their jackets tightly zipped.

"Look at the wake," Nicole said again, leaning closer to her friends this time. The smallest of the three, she looked like she was in danger of being blown off the deck.

Behind the ferry, two ribbons of white fanned out in a giant V. A nearby fishing boat bobbed as the first wave reached it.

"This ship is huge," Sue marvelled, shaking her head.

"We're on the *Queen of Surrey*," Nicole told her. "It weighs almost 7000 tonnes. That's like 1400 elephants." When Sue and Gina looked at her strangely, she shrugged, her black curls bouncing against her shoulders. "I read it on the sign inside."

"Of course you did," Sue said. Nicole read everything and seemed to remember every word.

"I can't believe it floats," Gina muttered, looking down toward the water.

"You should be saying 'Eureka!'" Nicole teased.

"Excuse me?"

"Eureka!" she said again. "That's what Archimedes said when he discovered water displacement. They say he was sitting in the bathtub at the time."

"Archi-who-des?" Sue asked.

"I can't believe you haven't heard that. You might have to be kicked out of the Science Squad for lack of theoretical knowledge," Nicole teased. Of course, the three girls weren't an official club. But they were all members of CAGIS—the Canadian Association for Girls in Science—and they had stumbled into so many mysteries that the kids at school started calling them the Science Squad. The name stuck.

Nicole was about to tell them about Archimedes when the loudspeakers crackled to life. "Your attention please. Gina Rossi, please report to the chief steward's office next to the cafeteria entrance."

Sue and Nicole raised their eyebrows, wondering what the chief steward could possibly want with Gina. There was no time to ask, however. Gina had already turned to go inside. Her friends hurried to follow.

The chief steward met them at the office with a smile that was more relaxed than his starched uniform. "Thanks for your letter," he said to Gina.

Sue and Nicole looked at each other again. "Letter?"

Gina explained as they followed the man up a narrow flight of stairs. "I wrote to BC Ferries about CAGIS and asked for a bridge tour."

Before they could ask more questions, Sue and Nicole found themselves shaking hands with the captain, a tall woman with flecks of grey in her hair.

"We thought you girls might be interested in seeing the ship's navigation systems."

The three nodded together, already staring at the banks of computers.

"We use a few different types of radar here," she continued. "This type you'll probably recognize. The hood shields the screen from the light. If you rest your face against it, you can take a look inside."

Sue leaned over and peered in. She found a black background with a line sweeping around it. Tiny blips were scattered across the screen.

"It looks like I'm in a submarine movie," she whispered.

After allowing the other two girls a chance to look, the captain moved to a second screen, which she called the daylight viewing radar. Yellow outlines showed the land, and Gina guessed that the smaller dots were boats. She peered out the windows of the bridge, trying to match the image on the screen with the scene around them.

"So this is how you keep from hitting anything?" she asked.

"We use our eyes as well." The captain smiled at her.

"What if it's foggy?" Nicole asked, still absorbed in the radar screen.

"Then the screens become more important. We also have our compass." She motioned toward a complicated-looking piece of equipment on its own stand. "This is called a Polaris."

"Can you see underwater as well?" asked Nicole.

"Well, we can't actually *see* under the water, but we have another computer that shows us the depth of the ocean. It's similar to radar, but it's called sonar." The captain pointed to a line moving

ARCHIMEDES

Nicole obviously knew about Archimedes's discovery. Archimedes was a Greek inventor, mathematician, and physicist who lived 2000 years ago. He came up with a number of principles and inventions such as the Archimedes screw and the Archimedes claw. Some of his most famous work has to do with water displacement and buoyancy. Archimedes's work in water displacement started when Hiero II, the king of Syracuse, gave Archimedes a difficult task. Hiero had paid for a crown to be made of solid gold. After the job was done, the king suspected that the goldsmith had replaced some of the gold with an equal weight of silver. Hiero asked Archimedes to figure out whether his suspicions were true. The tricky part was that Archimedes had to do this without damaging the crown in any way.

One day, as Archimedes was climbing into his bathtub, the water overflowed. "Eureka!" (which means "I found it") Archimedes cried; he had figured out how to determine whether the goldsmith had used silver in the gold crown! What Archimedes had figured out was the amount of water an object displaces (or moves) is equal to the volume of (the amount of space occupied by) the object. It is easy to figure out the volume of simple objects like cubes; one simply multiplies the length by the width by the height: $V = L \times w \times h$. But we can't do that with more complicated objects like crowns.

Archimedes's idea also had to do with the densities of different substances. Silver and gold have different densities: silver is less dense than gold. If the goldsmith had replaced some of the gold in the crown with an equal mass of silver, the silver would take up more space (have a bigger volume) than the removed gold because silver is less dense. All Archimedes had to do was take a quantity of pure gold of equal mass to the crown and determine whether their volumes (the pure gold and the crown) were the same, or whether the crown had a greater volume. If the crown did have a greater volume than the pure gold, he would know that the goldsmith had replaced some of the gold with silver because silver takes up more space per unit volume than gold.

How did Archimedes do this? With water, of course! Archimedes took his block of gold, which was equal in mass to the crown, and put it into a pail. He filled the pail to the brim with water. He then removed the block of gold from the pail of water. The water level in the pail dropped slightly when he removed the gold because it was no longer displacing the water in the pail. His next step was to put the crown into the same pail of water. If the crown was a mixture of silver and gold, the water in the pail would rise to the top and *overflow* because the crown would have taken up more space (had a greater volume) and displaced more water than the pure gold. If the crown was pure gold, the water level in the pail would have risen to the top of the pail just as it had when the pure gold block was in the water. It would not have overflowed since they both would have been of equal mass and equal volume.

What did Archimedes find? Although some people doubt the truth of the story, Archimedes apparently concluded that the goldsmith had in fact replaced some of the gold with silver and had defrauded the king.

For more information:

http://www.mcs.drexel.edu/~crorres/Archimedes/
   Crown/CrownIntro.html

slowly across the screen. "This draws us a picture of the ocean floor. Right now it's getting slightly more shallow."

Suddenly Sue pointed out the window. "I think I see the ferry dock."

"You're right," the captain nodded. "That's the city of Nanaimo. You girls will want to head down to Deck Five if you're walking off the boat."

DENSITY

Density is an important concept to understand. It helps explain why something as huge and heavy as the *Queen of Surrey* floats, and something as small as a marble can sink. Density is the mass per unit volume of a substance. The mass (m) of an object is the amount of matter it contains. (Remember from *Science Squad #1* that everything is made up of matter, and that matter is made up of molecules.) Mass is measured in kilograms (kg) or pounds (lbs.). It is in fact your mass you are measuring when you step on to a scale, not your weight! The volume (v) is the amount of space occupied by the object. Volume is measured in cubed metres (m^3) or litres (L). If we represent density as P, we can express it with the formula $P = m/v$. The unit used to measure density is kg/m^3, which is the unit for mass over the unit for volume, just like in the formula.

Every substance has a different density. That means if you were to take two different solids, liquids, or gases of equal volume, one could be heavier than the other. You can try this

• • •

Once they found the right exit and joined the crowd waiting there, Sue grinned at Gina. "That was great! I know I tease you about being too organized, but this time your planning paid off!"

Gina smiled, but Sue could tell she was already worrying about something else.

"Are you sure your Aunt Rose is okay with all of us visiting?"

yourself: take two identical paper or Styrofoam cups. Fill one with water. Fill another to the same height with sand. Which is heavier? The one filled with sand is much heavier, of course. Why? It is *denser* than the cup of water. The cup containing the sand is *heavier per unit volume* than the cup of water. What if we were to keep the mass constant instead? Let's go back to the water and sand example. Now start removing sand from the cup until it is just as heavy as the cup of water. What happened? The volumes are different now! You have much more water in the cup than sand. Since the sand is denser than the water, it is heavier per unit volume than the water. When we made the masses equal, the volume of the water had to be much greater than the volume of the sand to accommodate the difference in densities.

For more information:

http://pbskids.org/zoom/sci/h2odensity.html

"Definitely," Sue told her, digging into one of her backpack pockets. "Look—I've got her letter right here."

She handed it to Gina, who unfolded the paper and read it aloud.

Dear Sue:

As your mom's probably told you, my uncle—your great uncle—passed away this summer. He's left me some land on Vancouver Island, near Tofino. It's amazing here— really green and lush. There's a cabin on the property, right in the middle of old-growth forest.

There are some complications with the will, so I'll be staying here for a while. Maybe forever! I'm liking it better than my old city life in Vancouver. Why don't you and your friends join me for the last week of your vacation? It would be nice to have some company. And bring your bikes …

Hope to see you soon!
Love, Rose

"Is she really a carpenter?" Nicole asked.

Sue nodded. "She builds furniture, including these wacky twig chairs. I love them, but my mom calls them throwbacks to the hippie era."

"Why did she sign the letter Rose instead of Aunt Rose?" Gina wondered.

"Because she doesn't seem old enough to be an aunt. She's my mom's youngest sister. You'll see for yourself in a minute." The line started to move, and soon the girls were trailing outside into a parking lot.

"There she is!"

The woman Sue pointed out *was* young—maybe in her late twenties. She had the same blonde hair and freckles as Sue, and she was waving at them exuberantly.

"I see that your energy level is genetic," Gina said, rolling her eyes. Sue was already hugging Rose, and the two were bouncing up and down at the same speed.

When they pried themselves apart, Nicole offered her hand to Rose and found herself being hugged enthusiastically. Gina got the same treatment.

The group stopped at the baggage counter to pick up the girls' bikes and Sue's surfboard. Then they were off.

The drive from the ferry terminal to Tofino was almost three hours long, but there was so much to talk about that the time passed quickly. The girls told Rose about their summer adventures, from the pickpocket at the aquarium that Sue caught on film, to the passport they found in a field near Nicole's house.

"A passport? Whose?" Rose asked.

"It belonged to a backpacker at the hostel down the street," Nicole told her. "The poor guy was panicked when we finally found him. I guess when you take a nap in a field, you should make sure your backpack's zipped up!"

Rose laughed with the rest of them. Then she told the girls about her summer.

"You would have liked my uncle. He was an eccentric guy. I heard that he made his living as a rum smuggler along the coast, sneaking rum into the United States when alcohol was illegal there."

Sue's eyes widened. "I never heard that!"

"I guess it's a family secret," Rose grinned. "It always seemed strange to me because the rum runners worked on small boats in dangerous waters. My uncle couldn't swim."

"Weird," Sue agreed.

"He loved practical jokes. Once, some friends and I were camping on his property. We were sitting around the campfire late at night when we started hearing these groans and creaks. We'd been telling ghost stories, so we all freaked out! It turned out to be my uncle, hiding in the bushes. You can make really creepy noises with a string greased with violin resin. He was ninety when he passed away, and he still had his sense of humour."

"So was the inheritance a joke?" Gina asked.

"No. It's a puzzle, though. The will says that I now own fifty hectares of old-growth forest. It's mine as long as I don't subdivide it or use it for commercial purposes."

"What does that mean?"

"It means I can't log it or sell it off to developers."

"You wouldn't want to log it anyway, would you?"

"Of course not. But now that it's mine, I have to pay thousands of dollars in property taxes. And I don't have that kind of money." Rose shook her head. "That's nothing for you to worry about. You're going to have other things to do—I've booked some activities to keep you busy."

"What?" Sue asked quickly.

"Well, one of them involves a compass and a cute instructor."

"Seriously?"

"Seriously."

"What else have you planned?"

Rose smirked mischievously. "I don't think I'll tell you quite yet. It's good to have a few surprises."

"Come on!" Sue protested. "Tell us."

"Nope. There's no time, anyway. We're here!" ★

DENSITY EXPERIMENT

Some say that the method Archimedes used to measure whether the crown was pure gold or not was not precise enough to do the job. This is another method he could have used.

Materials:
- metal coat hanger
- plastercine
- playdough
- three pieces of string (each about 30 cm long)
- a large sink or bathtub (at least as wide as the coat hanger)

Procedure:

1. Think of the coat hanger as a triangle with the hook part coming out of the top of the triangle. We are going to be working with the top of the triangle in this step. Take your coat hangerand one of the three strings. The coat hanger is going to act as a balance so it is important that the centre string is exactly centred. To do this, fold the string in half bringing the two ends of the string together. This makes a loop at one end. Place the top of the triangle on top of the looped end of the string. Take the two ends of the string and pull one around each side of the hanger hook so the top of the triangle is right between them. Pull the two ends through the loop. Pull tight. Now, when you hold on to the two ends of the string, it should be in the exact centre of the coat hanger (see diagram on page 24).

2. Tie the other two strings at each end of the coat hanger (you can use a regular double knot for this), ensuring that the strings are the same length. Your balance is now ready.

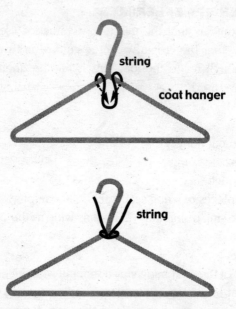

3. Make two balls, one of just plastercine, the other with a mix of playdough and plastercine. Try to make them about equal in mass. (You will probably have to make the mixed ball a bit bigger.)

4. Now tie one ball to one end of the hanger and the other ball to the other end of the hanger, again making sure the strings are the same length. The strings should also be nice and tight so the balls won't fall off. You can let the string sink into the playdough and plastercine as you pull the strings tight.

5. Hold your hanger by the centre string to test the masses of the two balls. (Make sure that the strings holding the two balls are still at the very ends of the coat hanger.) If the hanger is leaning to one side or the other, that ball is a bit heavier than the other. Add and remove plastercine and playdough until the hanger is balanced.

6. Fill the sink until the water is about 15–20 cm deep.

7. Hold up your balanced coat hanger from the centre string and slowly lower the balls hanging from the hanger into the water. Watch the hanger carefully as you do this. What happened? Is the hanger still balanced? Is it tilting to one side?

What Happened?

When you dipped the two balls into the water, the coat hanger should have tilted toward the ball made only of plastercine. Why was the hanger balanced in air, but not in water? Something else was working on the two balls when you dipped them into water: buoyancy. Whenever an object is submerged in a fluid (we used water), the object experiences an upward force, called the buoyant force. Archimedes's principle states that the buoyant force on an object is equal to the weight of fluid that object displaces. Since the mixed ball has a higher volume, it displaces more fluid and has a higher buoyant force. The buoyant force is an upward force on the object, so if the mixed ball has more of an upward force than the plastercine ball, it will tilt the coat-hanger balance toward the other denser ball. Archimedes could have tried this same experiment by tying the crown to one end of the balance and an equal mass of pure gold to the other end. He would then know if the crown was pure gold or not.

2

Where There's a Will...

Rose turned off the highway onto a winding gravel track, taking them into the shade of the cedars. Ferns swayed in from the sides of the road. Within a few minutes, a log cabin appeared, almost camouflaged against the forest.

"Wait," Rose called as the girls piled out of the truck and headed for the front door.

"I want to show you something first." She led them down a short trail, stopping in front of one of the giant tree trunks. Swinging from the branches above was a rope ladder.

"Cool!" Sue grabbed the rungs immediately. "Can I climb it?"

At Rose's nod, she quickly scurried up. At the top she found a tiny platform and a contraption on a cord. It took her only a second to figure out what it was.

"Can I try it?" she called.

FORCE

The simple definition of a force is a push or pull. Force refers to all sorts of pushes and pulls—like Gina picking up her backpack and the engine pushing Rose's truck. Forces speed things up, slow things down, and push things around corners and up hills. Forces can also distort matter by compressing, stretching, or twisting it. These common examples of force all involve motion, but motion does not need to occur for force to exist. Sue can exert a force by pushing on a wall, but Sue is not going to move the wall. So a force can cause motion, but it does not *always* cause motion. The unit used to measure force is the newton (named after Sir Isaac Newton). Force is often measured with a spring balance that is calibrated in newtons.

Throughout history, people have found ways to increase force and change the direction of force. A machine is a device that uses force. Although a machine can produce and control the direction of force, it cannot create energy. For a machine to work, it has to use energy, which can be human energy (like you pedalling your bicycle), electrical energy (like kitchen appliances), fossil fuel energy (see pp. 90–91 in *Science Squad #1*), solar, wind, or water energy.

For more information:

http://www.fi.edu/qa97/spotlight3/spotlight3.html
http://www.necc.mass.edu/MRVIS/MR3_13/
  start.htm#project

"Sure," Rose answered, her head emerging at the top of the ladder. "Just make sure you use the harness."

With her aunt's help, Sue was soon buckled into the safety straps. She grabbed the bar with both hands. Taking a deep breath, she pushed off the platform and sailed out from the tree. It was a zip line—a handlebar and harness attached to a cable strung far above the ground. Once she cleared the first thick branches, she saw Gina and Nicole below—and she heard Gina scream.

"Are you crazy?"

Before Sue could answer, she had arrived at the other side— a huge wooden platform balanced between the trunks of three trees. There was a railing for safety. Wide branches above kept it shady and dry.

Sue removed the harness and Rose slowly pulled the bar back to the other platform. A few minutes later, Gina landed in a flurry of black hair with her arms spread wide for balance. She looked breathless, like she couldn't believe what she had just done.

Sue grinned at her. For cautious Gina, this must have seemed like a life-threatening activity. At fourteen, Gina was two years older than her best friends. Most of the time, she seemed to think that made her two years wiser. It was unusual to see her flustered.

"I think this is called a zip line," Sue said, trying to sound casual. "I've seen one before at an adventure park."

Within a few minutes, both Nicole and Rose had joined them on the platform.

"This is awesome!" Nicole raved, examining the cables closely. "Where do you buy something like this?"

"I made it," Rose answered. When all three girls turned to stare at her, she shrugged. "I've been here all summer. Until people started ordering my furniture, I had lots of time on my hands."

With her audience captive, Rose showed the girls how the zip

28

line worked. There was a pulley at each end, and the cable glided between them. After she had quizzed them and watched them each practise fastening the harness, she was satisfied that the girls could use it safely on their own.

Before they left, the girls explored every inch of the platform, from the hand-hewn railings to the bird's nest in the branches high above. Nicole took a last look around and gave a firm nod, sending her dark curls bouncing. "I hereby declare this the official Science Squad headquarters for the rest of our vacation!"

On the way back down the trail, Rose had one more lesson for her guests. She showed them the moss and lichens on the rocks alongside the trail. She pointed to the roots of the cedars, which twisted over the path.

"The biking's great around here, but muddy," she said.

"No worries," Sue told her. "I can weave around mud puddles like a race car driver."

"That's exactly what I'm worried about. The more you weave around the puddles, the wider the trail gets. And the wider the trail gets, the more of these plants we kill."

"So...no weaving?" Gina offered.

"Exactly."

When they had made their way back to the cabin, the girls found the front porch a maze of twig chairs and twig tables. The branches were woven so skilfully that the furniture almost seemed alive.

"Cool!" Nicole exclaimed, studying them.

"It's gotten a bit out of control, I'm afraid," Rose said modestly. "I've discovered there's a lot more demand for this type of furniture here than there was in the city. I have orders coming out my ears! I've rented some workspace in town and it looks like I'm going to be busier than I expected for the next little while."

PULLEYS

Rose used the physics of simple machines to make the zip line. A pulley, a type of simple machine, consists of a grooved wheel that turns around an axle. A rope fits into the groove and moves around it. There are different types of pulleys (see diagram). A simple pulley is fixed in one place, firmly attached by an axle. One end is attached to a load like a basket. The rope goes up and loops over the pulley and comes down. This type of pulley is useful if you want to change the direction of the force you have to apply. For example, say Sue wanted to lift a 10-kg basket a height of 3 m up to the tree platform. Sue could be on the platform and pull the basket up attached to a rope. If so, she would have to exert 9.8 N of force upward to lift the basket. (Remember, force is measured in newtons (N), and 9.8 N is the force corresponding to the 10-kg weight.) Or she could attach a pulley to a tree branch at a height higher than the platform and exert the same 9.8 N of force from the ground to pull up the basket. In both cases, she needs to exert 9.8 N of force to lift the basket, but Sue is changing the direction of the force when she stands on the ground. She is exerting a downward force when she is using the pulley.

A second type of pulley is a movable pulley, which moves along a rope. It gives a gain in force but a loss in distance. This means that you need to apply less force to lift the object, but you need to pull more rope a longer distance to get the object to the same height. If Sue attaches the basket onto the movable pulley as shown in the diagram, the weight of the basket ends up being suspended by two ropes, which splits the weight of the basket in two. Now each piece of rope holds 5 kg of weight, which means Sue only has to exert 4.9 N (9.8 ÷ 2) of force to lift

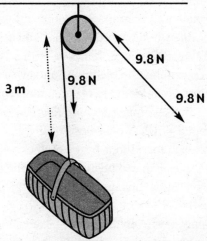

the basket. But if Sue wants to lift her basket 3 m to the tree platform, she would need 6 m of rope. So by using simple and movable pulleys together, she halves the force she needs to exert to
lift up the basket, but she needs double the length of rope to lift
it the same distance.

For more information:

http://www.howstuffworks.com/pulley.htm

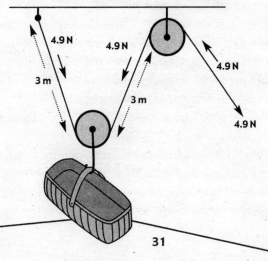

Sue gave her aunt a proud hug, then the girls proceeded inside and piled their things on the bunk beds in the spare bedroom. The little house was small but cozy, with a combined living room and kitchen, a miniature bathroom, and two small bedrooms.

Sue and Rose volunteered to make dinner. There was no TV, so Gina pulled a book—*Mysteries of the Rain Forest*—off the shelf, and Nicole flopped down on the floor near a pile of magazines. Flipping through, she found four pages of thick paper. They were curled at the edges as if they'd been rolled up. She began to read.

"Hey…this must be the uncle's will!"

Gina leaned over to look.

"The first page says everything Rose talked about," Nicole said quietly. " *No commercial usage…must remain individually owned by the recipient…* Why does legal stuff have to sound so…legal?"

Rose looked over the kitchen counter at them. "You found the original!" she said. " I knew I left that around here somewhere."

Nicole flipped to the second page. It was blank, except for a tiny page number hand-written at the bottom. The third and fourth pages were the same.

"Why the extra pages?" she asked.

Rose shrugged. "They were like that, all rolled up together."

Nicole held the pages up to the window, trying to see through them. They remained blank. "That's crazy," she muttered to herself. Who would put three blank pages in a will?"

Her musings were interrupted by a knock at the door.

"That must be Tyler," Rose called. "Would one of you mind grabbing the door?"

"Who's Tyler?" Gina asked Sue, who answered by making kissing noises from the other side of the kitchen counter.

"Sue! Stop that!" Rose swatted her with a tea towel. "His name is Tyler Riley, and he's just a friend. So far. Will someone let him in?"

Tyler was tall, tanned, and dressed like a surfer, the girls discovered when they finally opened the door. "Hey there. Welcome to the edge of the world, most gnarly place on earth," he greeted them.

Rose giggled, sounding much younger than she had earlier that day. "Isn't he hilarious?" she whispered to the girls, before greeting Tyler with a kiss. "Did you surf today?" she asked him.

"I thought about it, but the line-up was zoo'd today."

"Zoo'd?" Nicole said.

"Way too crowded, man."

• • •

Late that night, happily wrapped in layers of blankets on the top bunk, Gina yawned and said she could hardly keep her eyes open. But Sue and Nicole were wide awake on the bunks below her.

"He's cute," Nicole whispered.

"He's okay," Sue answered. "But what kind of person uses the word 'gnarly' in normal conversation?"

"Okay? He's not just okay. He's a surfer. He's totally good looking. *And* he's an environmental activist. That's perfect for Rose."

"Don't bet on it," Sue told her. "Rose has got terrible taste in men. Besides, he doesn't seem that smart."

"What do you mean?"

"When Gina asked him about endangered species in the rain forest, he didn't know much."

Hearing her name, Gina peered down. "It's true," she yawned. "I believe his exact words were 'There are some primo lookin' critters around here, dude.'"

Her imitation of Tyler's surfer drawl made them crack up.

"Seriously," Gina insisted. "When I asked him for examples, he changed the subject."

"That's weird. I didn't think about it before, but he didn't know anything about lichens, either." Even in the dark, Sue could see Nicole wrinkle her forehead, the way she did when she was thinking hard.

"Lichens? Why would anyone have to know about lichens?" Sue asked.

"I read that they're sensitive to pollution. If there are lichens growing somewhere, you know the environment's doing well."

"Is that true?"

Nicole shrugged, creating a rustling of blankets in the dark. "Tyler didn't seem to know."

"Tyler doesn't know much," Sue grumbled. "And did you see

RAIN FORESTS

 Gina pulled a book off the shelf called *Mysteries of the Rain Forest*. She would have read that a tropical rain forest has tall, broad-leaved, densely growing trees and a wet climate. Rain forests are more commonly found in the tropics and sub-tropics, but some rain forests exist in cooler, temperate zones like the coastal areas of British Columbia. Coastal temperate rain forests, such as the Pacific Rim National Park near Tofino where Rose lives, have large and very old trees (old growth) with needles. Some trees in temperate rain forests are more than 2000 years old and are wider than six metres in diameter! Around the world, coastal rain forests are rare. Of the 1.3 billion hectares of temperate rain forest that exist around the world, only 30–40 million hectares (2–3 percent) are coastal temperate rain forest.

Both tropical and temperate rain forests contain a great variety of plant, animal, and insect species. This variety of plant how long he looked at the will? He seemed to think that if he stared at the blank pages long enough, words would appear. I don't see why Rose showed them to him in the first place."

"That's ridiculous. I'm sure Tyler's a perfectly nice person, even if he isn't that smart. Now can we please get some sleep?" Gina flopped back onto her pillow.

"Okay," Sue agreed. "And you're right—Tyler might be a nice person. But until we know for sure, I'm not going to trust him."

The other two nodded. "Agreed." ★

and animal life is called biological diversity or biodiversity. It has been estimated that tropical rain forests contain more than half the world's species even though they occupy only 7 percent of the earth's land area. Coastal temperate rain forests collect and store huge amounts of organic matter like wood, leaves, moss, other living plants, and soil. In fact, coastal temperate rain forests store more organic matter than any other type of forest including tropical rain forests. Because rain forests are the richest regions on earth in terms of biological diversity, the preservation of rain forests is very important.

For more information:

http://www.rainforestweb.org/Rainforest_Information/
   Sites_for_Kids/

http://www.EnchantedLearning.com/subjects/
   rainforest/Allabout.shtml

http://www.inforain.org/rainforestatlas/index.htm

http://www.raincoastadventures.com/

http://www.carefreeenterprise.com/vancouver/

ZIP LINE ENGINEERING EXPERIMENT

Rose constructed the zip line from a movable pulley that travels along a rope. Each end of the rope is attached to an anchored vertical structure, like a tree or tower. One end of the rope is positioned lower than the other end so that the rope has a small decline. Because the rope is sloped downward, the pulley moves down the rope. You can make your own small zip line.

Materials:

* an empty sewing machine bobbin
* a large metal paper clip
* a metre-long piece of heavy string about 2–3 mm thick
* small paper gift bag with handles, or a small basket

Procedure:

1. With pliers, open up the paper clip at the smaller-sized bend to form an "S" shape as shown in the diagram.
2. Insert the wider end of the paper clip through the bobbin and have the bobbin rest on the bottom of the loop as shown in the diagram.
3. With pliers, bend the end of the paper clip up over the bobbin so that the bobbin is secure. This is your *pulley*.
4. Tie one end of your string to the back of a chair or a door knob.
5. Hook the bag onto the pulley.
6. Thread the string between the bobbin and paper clip.
7. Hold the end of the string so the string is tight and the bobbin is resting on the string.
8. Hold the string at an angle and watch your pulley move the bag down the string.

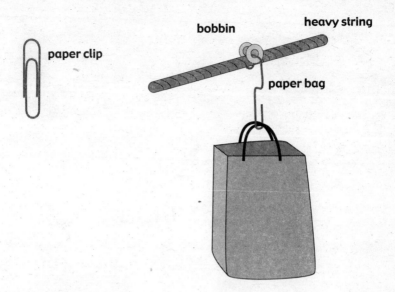

paper clip

bobbin　**heavy string**

paper bag

What Happened?

By making and using a pulley to move the bag along the string, you've made a zip line. By holding the string at an angle, the force of gravity caused the pulley to move down the string.

For more information:

http://www.brightwoodranch.ca/webpages/
  large%20photos/zipline.htm

http://www.greatoakscamp.org/zipline.htm

http://users.ev1.net/~mwatson/unit/scout/sshow2000/
  zl.htm

3

Trail and Tricks

"Rose sure knows how to choose an instructor," Sue whispered to Gina, arching an eyebrow mischievously.

The man facing them was in his early twenties, with shaggy black hair that he brushed away from his eyes. "My name is Chris, and Rose has asked me to teach you everything there is to know about orienteering." He had an Australian accent. When he wasn't looking, Sue pretended to swoon. Gina rolled her eyes.

"That's finding directions, right?" Nicole asked.

"Exactly right, mate." As he talked, Chris sat on a rock and pulled maps and compasses out of his backpack. Gina looked around, wondering which way he was going to lead them. Rose had dropped them off with their bikes at an entrance to Pacific Rim National Park, and even though it was not actually raining, the forest looked damp. At one side, the ground dropped toward a small creek, and she wrinkled her nose as the smell of skunk cabbage drifted up.

"Come and sit close to the map, and I'll explain some of the symbols," Chris said. Sue was immediately perched at his side. He spread a brightly coloured map on the ground and began pointing to features. "The things in black are manmade—things like bridges, roads, and trails."

"How did you learn all this?" Sue asked, still looking like she might melt.

"I travelled around the world for a few years. Came here to hike the West Coast Trail, and I met another Aussie who was running a guiding company. Been here ever since," he grinned.

"You just decided to stay?"

"That's the way Tofino is. Plenty of space, plenty of surfing, and no reason to leave. Folks have washed up here from all parts of the world."

Turning back to his map, he pointed out more details. "The lines in brown are the topographical features."

"The what?" Sue shook her head.

"Topographical," Nicole repeated before Chris could answer. "They mark the elevation. When they're far apart, it means the land is flat. When they're close together, there could be a cliff."

Chris nodded at her, impressed.

"How do you know all that, Einstein?" Sue asked.

"The guides on our caving expedition last year had the same kind of map, with the cave openings marked on it. They showed me."

"Did they tell you anything about compasses?" Chris asked. Nicole shook her head.

"Well then, here we go."

Standing up, Chris showed them a path he had marked on the

39

ORIENTEERING

Sue, Gina, and Nicole are learning the sport of orienteering. They probably don't know that orienteering began in Scandinavia in the 1800s as a military exercise. The modern version of orienteering didn't start as a competitive sport until 1919 in Sweden. The Science Squad used a map and a compass to find their way across unfamiliar tracts of land, like the Pacific Rim National Park. A typical orienteering event is like playing a giant board game. The organizer places orange-and-white or red-and-white markers at different places found on their map. These markers are checkpoints along the course. The purpose of the sport is to use the map and compass to find the markers and return to the finish line. Orienteers try to use their navigational skills to choose the best route to each control marker. When they get to the marker, they mark a scorecard to show they reached it. You can do orienteering on foot, on skis, or on a bicycle, during the day or at night, but the purpose is the same: you use a map and compass to find your way across unfamiliar terrain.

For more information:

http://www.the-spa.com/tony.maniscalco/tryo.htm
http://www.map-reading.com/appendf.php

map. It led down the trail to the left, then swerved off to follow a stream. He handed the map to Nicole and showed her how to turn it to match the direction she was facing. Then he placed the clear compass over top of the map and helped her mark her direction.

"Now, let's see if you're right. When you find a turnoff, there will be a red and white ribbon to collect," he told them in his singsong accent. He pronounced ribbon "ree-bin."

Nicole, Sue, and Gina headed off down the path, Chris sauntering a few steps behind. He was quiet, waiting for them to make their own decisions. Nicole looked at the map, then studied the legend at the bottom.

"We're supposed to follow the trail for 200 metres," she said. "Have we gone 200 metres?"

Sue shrugged and Gina rolled her eyes, as if the whole exercise were useless. Nicole looked back at Chris, who didn't say anything.

"He'd be cuter if he talked," Nicole muttered.

Finally Gina leaned in to help study the map. "Look at the black signs. It's *obvious* there's a bridge where we leave the trail."

Nicole ignored her superior tone. "Have we passed a bridge?"

They all looked back down the trail. And saw that Chris was standing on a wooden boardwalk over a dry stream bed—a small bridge they had walked over without noticing.

Unhappy that she had missed the turn, Nicole stomped back and climbed down to the streambed. She popped up a moment later, waving a red and white ribbon.

"It was tied to a bush," she called.

Gina and Sue walked past a smug Chris and joined Nicole on the strip of rock and gravel. "So, we've turned left," she said. "Now we just follow this stream bed until it hits another trail, then follow that trail to the beach."

TOPOGRAPHICAL MAPS

Maps are critical for orienteering. Remember from pp. 136–137 and 139–143 of *Science Squad #1* that maps are two-dimensional representations of the physical features of land regions. These different physical features are represented by different colours and by various markings, called symbols. Some of the different colours represent different features. For example, black often represents human-made features like roads and buildings. Blue often represents water, like oceans, lakes, and rivers, while brown often identifies different elevations (heights). The symbols used on the map are displayed in a box on the map, called the legend. Some maps, like road maps, show roads, railway lines, rivers, and lakes. Other maps show topographical (or topographic—both terms are correct) features, meaning they show the shape of the land. These maps show the hills and valleys of the land region. Sue, Gina, and Nicole are using maps that show the topography of the park because they are the most useful type of map for outdoor activities.

For more information:

**http://www.enchantedlearning.com/geography/
  mapreading/**
http://www.map-reading.com/ch3-3.php

It didn't turn out to be that easy. In a few spots, bushes had reclaimed the stream bed, their prickly branches impossible to push through. The girls had to force their way around them.

When they got to the trail junction, the stream bed had sunk into a miniature canyon, and the other trail crossed on a bridge, far above them. If they had remembered to look at the topographical lines, they would have seen the change in elevation. Sighing, they retraced their path until they found a way up the side of the canyon. Then they bushwhacked back to intersect with the second trail.

Finally, Sue gave a happy shout. "I see sand! We made it!" Grabbing the compass from Nicole, she turned and tossed it back toward Chris. Then she ran for the beach. When Nicole and Gina caught up to her, she was pawing her way dramatically toward the ocean.

"Water," she rasped. "Water."

"Very funny," Gina said, crossing her arms over her chest. "This is not the desert. And it's salt water."

"Good point." Sue jumped up to brush the sand off herself. "You," she said, turning to Nicole, "are hereby awarded the number one rain forest navigation trophy." With a flourish, she presented Nicole with a piece of driftwood. She offered a second to Gina.

A loud clapping interrupted the festivities. "A smashing success," Chris said as he joined them. "You did a brilliant job. And you may keep the compass, as well as your trophies."

Shaking her head, Gina pointed her stick at him. "You were no help at all!"

Chris winked. "Would a ride home make it up to you?"

• • •

Back at the cabin, Gina and Sue peeled off their muddy boots before collapsing on the couch.

"I can't believe Nicole had the energy to go to the library," Sue said.

"I can't believe she went out in public looking like this!" Gina surveyed the muddy patches on her pants and claimed the first shower. A couple hours later, both girls were cleaned up and relaxing on the porch. Sue was dabbing sunscreen on her freckled skin when Nicole pedalled up the driveway.

She pulled an armload of books from her panniers and dumped them on the porch stairs. "When I chose all of these, I forgot that I

COMPASSES

Sue, Gina, and Nicole needed a compass for orienteering because it helped them determine their directions. Most compasses are magnetic and each one is made with a small, lightweight magnet in the shape of a pointer. This pointer is called a needle and is balanced in the middle like a teeter-totter so that it can rotate and move easily. One end of the needle is often labelled N (north) or is sometimes coloured to indicate that it points toward the north. The face of the compass is labelled with the letters N (north), E (east), S (south), and W (west). When the compass is held still, the pointer of the compass rotates until it is pointing toward the North Pole.

A magnetic compass works by using the earth's magnetic fields. You can think of the earth as having a huge bar magnet going up and down the centre between the North and had to bike home. I'm lucky my legs didn't fall off. And you wouldn't believe what I saw."

"A sasquatch? He probably thought you were a potential date." Laughing at her own joke, Gina leaned over to pick a twig out of Nicole's curls.

"Not a sasquatch. Tyler!"

"Ugh." Sue rolled her eyes. "I'd rather see a sasquatch."

"I was coming out of the library, and I saw Tyler walking down the street in front of me. I was about to shout hello when he took a last swallow out of his pop can and threw it away."

South Poles. Magnets have special properties. They can attract certain materials like iron (steel), nickel, and cobalt. Every magnet has a north and south pole. Two magnets sometimes attract and other times repel each other, depending on which poles are facing each other. The first law of magnetism states that opposite poles attract (north pulls on south) and similar poles repel each other (north pushes away north). In order for the north needle of a compass to point toward the North Pole, the huge bar magnet in the earth's centre has to have its south end at the North Pole.

For more information:

http://www.infoed.net/edusciencemag.htm
http://science.howstuffworks.com/compass.htm

"And?" Sue asked. "I don't get it."

Nicole gave her an impatient look. "What kind of environmental activist throws an aluminium can in the garbage?"

"I knew that guy was bad news," Sue said. "We should tell Rose and—"

Nicole interrupted her. "I'm sure Rose will be thrilled to find out I was spying on her boyfriend. And do you really think she'd stop seeing someone because of a pop can? Besides, I have more things to show you. I looked up Rose's uncle in a town history, and I found this biography."

Sue skimmed the entry. "*Mr. Jack Madison...eccentric...rum smuggler...practical joker...recluse in his later years...* This is exactly what Rose told us."

"Yes, but it got me thinking, and I went looking for books on practical jokes," Nicole told her. "There were only a few there, and this one still has an old sign-out card pasted inside, from before the library was computerized. It was signed out by Jack Madison three times."

"So?" Gina asked, leaning closer.

"So look at page 60."

Gina flipped to find the page while Sue leaned over her shoulder. "Page 50—fake blood. Page 56—how to make a UFO. Page 60—invisible ink."

Nicole nodded. "Right. Invisible ink. And invisible ink made me think of..."

Sue and Gina answered at the same time. "The will." ★

COMPASS EXPERIMENT

Sue, Gina, and Nicole need a compass for orienteering. If they didn't have one, this is a simple way they could make a compass.

Materials:
* a cork stopper from a wine or other bottle
* a short, thick, metal sewing needle like a darning needle
* a tin pie plate or casserole dish filled with about 4 cm of water
* a magnet

Procedure:
1. With a knife, carefully cut a round disc of cork about 4 mm thick.
2. Put one end of the sewing needle on the magnet for 10 seconds.
3. Float the cork disc in the bowl of water.
4. Lay the sewing needle on the floating cork disc. Don't let the needle touch the water.
5. Watch the needle stabilize and point in one direction.

What Happened?

The needle should act like a compass needle and point in the north–south direction. This occurred because you temporarily magnetized the needle, meaning that the needle developed a north and south pole. Remember the first law of magnetism states that opposite poles attract (north pulls on south) and similar poles repel each other (north pushes away from north). For the north needle of a compass to point toward the North Pole, the huge bar magnet in the earth's centre has to have its south end at the North Pole. This is why the north side of the needle was attracted to the North Pole.

4

Heating Things Up

When Rose swept into the cabin late in the afternoon, Nicole, Gina, and Sue began talking at the same time.

"He threw a pop can in the garbage. An aluminum pop can."

"The orienteering was cool. We got lost once, but—"

"Your uncle checked out a library book with instructions on invisible ink. That could explain the last three pages of the will."

Pulling a brush through her hair and grabbing a briefcase from beside the door, Rose was clearly short of time—and patience. "Look, I'm glad you had a good day, but I have to run. I have a meeting with a buyer in fifteen minutes. He wants to sell my furniture in stores in Victoria!"

"But what about Tyler?" Sue protested.

"Tyler may not be perfect, but I'm sure he doesn't make a habit of throwing away pop cans. And my uncle was strange, but not that strange. I doubt he'd write a legal document in invisible ink. I have to go. I'll be back at seven with dinner."

All three girls opened their mouths to start talking again, but she was gone before they could begin.

"Tyler *did* throw a pop can away," Nicole protested.

"We believe you," Gina comforted her.

"And the will *is* written in invisible ink. I'm sure of it."

This time Gina and Sue looked doubtful.

"I'll prove it. Didn't Rose say the pages I found yesterday were the originals?" Nicole began rummaging through the piles of magazines on the coffee table. Within a few moments, she surfaced with the will. Then she grabbed her library books and headed out the door, not waiting to see if the other two followed.

They did follow, of course. All three Science Squad members were soon settled on the tree platform to witness Nicole separate the pages of the will. She placed one in a patch of sunshine filtering through the branches.

Nothing happened. Gina and Sue were diplomatically silent.

Nicole growled in frustration and checked the instructions. "*Write your secret message in lemon juice and allow it to dry. To reveal your words, lay the paper on a sunny windowsill.* That's what we did!"

Sue smiled hesitantly. "It was worth a try."

Glaring at her, Nicole gathered the pages. "It's *still* worth a try. I'm going inside to check the Internet. I must be doing something wrong."

Once again, Gina and Sue trailed behind her.

Starting up Rose's laptop, Nicole wrinkled her forehead in concentration and typed "invisible ink" into the Internet search engine. She got 102,000 hits. There was a book about ghosts and an article on counterfeiting money. There was even a story about how

ALUMINUM

Why is aluminum used for pop cans? Because aluminum is light but strong and the most commonly found metal on earth. Aluminum is a silvery metal found in 8 percent of the earth's crust. It has a density of 2.70 g/cm^3 compared to gold, which has a density of 19.3 g/cm^3. In fact, aluminum has a lower density than most other metals. Remember from page 18 that density is the mass per unit volume. That means if you were to take equal volumes of gold and aluminum, the piece of gold would be much heavier than the piece of aluminum. Aluminum has other useful properties. Not only is it light and strong, but it is also malleable (meaning it can be hammered or pressed into different shapes without being broken) and a good conductor of electricity and heat. Aluminum has many uses. For example, Rose probably uses aluminum foil to wrap up foods in her kitchen. Power lines are made from aluminum because it conducts electricity so well. And aluminum is used for all kinds of products from ladders to bikes to airplanes.

What Rose and the Science Squad may not know is that they may even have jewellery made from aluminum compounds. Many gemstones like rubies and sapphires are made up mostly of crystalline aluminum oxide. Other gems containing aluminum are garnets, emeralds, and aquamarines. So now you have a quiz question for your friends: What is similar about pop cans and rubies? They both contain aluminum!

For more information:

http://www.bayerus.com/msms/fun/pages/periodic/ aluminum/

http://www.encyclopedia.com/html/a1/alumin.asp

spies once wrote in invisible ink between the lines of ordinary letters. Finally, halfway down the page, she found the link she was looking for.

This time, the instructions for revealing the ink were slightly different: *Write a note to your friends in invisible ink and allow the page to dry. Then ask an adult to help you hold the paper near a light bulb.*

"We did that. Nothing happened," Gina said.

Nicole disagreed. "We held the pages in the sunlight."

"Same thing, isn't it?" Sue asked. Her limited attention span was clearly running out.

"Nope. A light bulb doesn't produce just light."

"Heat!" Understanding suddenly lit Gina's eyes. "Let's turn on a lamp." Gina inspected the lamp in the corner of the living room and discovered that she could easily remove the shade. She held her hand over the top. "I think it's getting warm. Give me the first page."

Nicole handed it over and Gina held the top corner close to the bulb, being careful not to burn it. She held her breath. Sue was hopping up and down with impatience. After a minute, Gina lifted the paper.

"It's there! I can see words!"

"I knew it!" Nicole shouted. "Keep going." Grabbing another page of the will, she headed for a bedroom lamp. Sue quickly did the same, although she had trouble holding the paper still enough.

Within a few minutes, the girls were looking at three complete pages, written in the spidery scrawl that they recognized from the first page of the will.

"We've done it!" Nicole gloated.

"We've revealed them," Gina said, "but they're complete gibberish."

INVISIBLE INK

Cryptography is the study of hidden messages. It comes from the Greek words "kryptos," meaning hidden, and "graphen," meaning to write. Hidden messages can be written in code that needs to be decoded. Or they can be concealment messages, meaning they are just hidden. Invisible ink is a good example of a concealment message.

Throughout history, invisible ink has made it possible to send and receive secret messages. Invisible ink has been used by spies, by people during wartime, and by people in prison. For example, during the Nazi occupation of Poland in the Second World War, all mail sent out of Poland was being read by the Nazis. The Polish could not write openly about the war because the Nazis wanted to keep their harsh treatment of the Polish people a secret from the rest of the world. The Nazis saw nothing unusual about a postcard with a typical one-sentence greeting. What they didn't realize was that the postcard also contained a message written in invisible ink! This message asked for supplies, including invisible ink, and described the awful things happening in Poland. Invisible ink had made it possible for the news to be secretly sent out.

For more information:

http://www.cs.usask.ca/resources/tutorials/csconcepts/
  encryption/Lessons/L1/History.html

http://chemistry.about.com/c/ht/02/12/
  How_Invisible_Ink_1039299060.htm

http://www.scienceyear.com/outthere/parents/SpyBox.pdf

The first page seemed to be a chart. It was roughly rectangular and filled with small squares. Two of the squares, near opposite ends of the chart, were slightly shaded.

Nicole shook her head slowly, her curls dropping over her face as she leaned closer to the chart. "I have no idea what this is," she admitted.

The next page was a map. It had curving topographical lines that the girls recognized from their orienteering session. Letters ran along the top edge and the left-hand side.

"There's no X to mark the spot," Sue whispered.

"We couldn't find X anyway," Gina said. "This could be a map of Brazil for all we know."

The third page didn't look at all scientific. It was more like an illustration. Something suddenly clicked in Sue's head, and she turned to look over the kitchen counter. "Hey! This sketch is of Rose's kitchen window."

Turning to look, Gina and Nicole saw that she was right. The illustration was a perfect copy of the window, including the wooden sill and the empty curtain rod at the top. The illustrator had shaded in a few rays of sunshine on the other side of the glass.

This time, when Rose walked in the door, the girls were prepared. They were leaning in a row against the kitchen counter, each holding one page. Rose didn't seem to have slowed down since she left. She flung open the door and held it open with her foot while dropping her briefcase, her purse, and two pizza boxes inside.

"Would it be possible to get a little help around here?" She sighed, leaning down to untie her shoes. None of the girls moved.

"Hello? Have you been turned into stone?"

Slowly, Nicole turned over the first page of the will so that Rose could see it.

"What's that?"

Nicole didn't answer, and Gina slowly turned her page over. "Is that what I think it is?"

Grinning, Sue flipped the final page. "We did it! Well, Nicole did it, really. She thought the last three pages of the will were written in invisible ink, and they were!"

"What do they say?" Rose practically snatched the first page out of Nicole's hand and scanned it eagerly. Then her face dropped. "This makes no sense."

Sue admitted that they hadn't been able to understand the pages, either. "I'm sure we'll think of something, though. It must be a code of some kind...."

She was interrupted by a knock at the door. Tyler swung it open himself before waiting for anyone to answer. He was dressed in shorts and a Hawaiian shirt, like he'd just ridden a wave from Maui.

"I thought I'd come by and see if anyone is free for dinner. Is that some za I smell? Primo! Hey, what are those pages?"

Without waiting for an answer, he sauntered into the room and looked over Rose's shoulder. "Is that the will? You must be stoked! How did you find it?"

Rose seemed to be beyond speaking. She just shook her head and put the page down beside the couch. "This is just too much to think about right now. Let's have some dinner. Tyler, you're welcome to join us for pizza."

"Primo," he said. Rose led the way into the kitchen and the girls followed. But when Sue glanced back, Tyler had gathered all three pages of the will and was examining them closely. He seemed to be counting the squares of the chart on the first page.

"Look," she hissed to Gina. "He's snooping at our will."

Tyler looked up with a start to find the two girls watching him. "Hey, Rose?" he called. "Mind if I trace these? I'll see if I can scope out some answers for you."

"Sure," Rose said.

Sue's jaw dropped, and she could only gla slipped by her, smiling. ★

INVISIBLE WRITING EXPERIMENT

There are a number of ways to write secret messages and one way is with water. A watermark is a faint or invisible imprint on paper that can be seen by holding the paper up to light or by making it wet.

Materials:

✳ a number of pieces of thin white paper

✳ water

✳ a hard leaded pencil

✳ a box of watercolours with paintbrush

Procedure:

1. Run a piece of paper under water in the sink to make it thoroughly wet.
2. Place it on a hard, smooth, waterproof surface, such as a kitchen counter.
3. Cover the wet piece of paper with a dry piece of paper.
4. Write a message with the hard pencil on the dry piece of paper, making sure to press firmly when you are writing your message.
5. Recycle the dry piece of paper.
6. Hold the wet piece of paper up to the light and observe.
7. Let the piece of paper dry.
8. To make the writing visible, wet the piece of paper again and brush a thin layer of watercolour paint over the paper.

t Happened?

When you wrote your message, you pressed the fibres down hard on the dry piece of paper, which made a watermark on the wet paper. The fibres were pushed down lower than the top surface, making an indentation. Because the surface of the paper was not smooth, light was reflected differently when you held it up to the light or when you made it wet again and used the watercolours.

5

Surf's Up

Nicole had just fallen asleep when Sue and Gina shook her back to consciousness.

"What are you doing?" she muttered, trying to tug the blankets over her head. Gina pulled them away.

"We're having an emergency Science Squad meeting," Sue whispered. "We've got to decode those pages before Tyler does. We're going to the tree platform so we don't wake up Rose."

"Great. Go without me." Nicole tried to grab her blankets back, but Gina held them firmly.

"We're not going without you. We need your brain, encyclopedia girl."

With a groan—which Gina immediately shushed—Nicole rolled out of bed and pulled a sweatshirt and jeans over her cotton pyjamas.

"This inheritance better be worth it," she grumbled as she followed the beam of Gina's flashlight out of the cabin and down the trail. Sue had brought some candles, so once all three girls had made it across the zip line, the platform was actually quite cozy.

While Gina spread out the papers, Nicole leaned back to see the stars through the moving branches.

"It's so peaceful here," she whispered. "All I can hear is the rustle of those papers and you two breathing." Just as she stopped talking, a branch snapped.

"What was that?" she said, springing up. "Did you hear that?" Gina and Sue nodded, their eyes wide in the candlelight. "Shhh," Sue said. "Let's see if we hear it again."

They stayed perfectly still. For a minute, there was no sound. Then they heard a rustle from the branches.

"What is it?" Nicole breathed.

"It sounds like it's right above us," Sue answered.

Gina turned her flashlight onto the tree. At first, they saw only green. Then the beam swept past something else. "It's that bird's nest we saw."

"I thought that was empty," Nicole said uncertainly. Even as she said it, two sets of gleaming eyes appeared in the light.

"Owls," Gina whispered. As their eyes adjusted, the girls could make out two large birds.

"Give me some paper," Gina motioned to Sue. "I'm going to draw them and maybe we can identify them tomorrow."

For the next fifteen minutes, Gina sketched quickly, trying to capture large round eyes, light chest feathers, and gently speckled wings. Nicole held up a couple of the candles, allowing just enough light for Gina to see but not enough to scare the birds.

"We're wasting time," Sue complained, wiggling impatiently. "We're supposed to be decoding the will." Then one of the owls

STARS

Nicole is enjoying the stars. She probably knows that stars are huge balls of burning gases that look very small because they are very far away. The star closest to the earth is the sun. Even though it is a medium-sized star, it looks big because it is a lot closer to the earth (150 million kilometres away) than other stars. The sun has been shining for about 4500 million years and will continue to do so for about another 4500 million years before any real changes occur.

Stars go through various stages during their long cycle of birth and death. They are formed inside huge clouds of gas and dust called a nebula. For a star to be formed, the particles of gas within the nebula must collapse to form clumps of matter. These clumps are pulled tighter and smaller by their own gravity. As the densities (see p. 18 for a description of density) of the clumps increase, the temperature at the core (centre) also increases. Most of the gas in a star is hydrogen. In the star's core, hydrogen reaches the temperature of 10 million degrees Celsius. The heat in the core of the star causes hydrogen to change into helium, which causes an atomic reaction. This atomic reaction generates energy and the billions of atomic reactions that occur generate light and heat from the stars.

For more information:

**http://imagine.gsfc.nasa.gov/docs/science/know_l2/
   stars.html**

http://www.astro.wisc.edu/~dolan/constellations/

turned to look at her, and she held her breath. For the next few minutes, she managed to stay almost perfectly still. With the occasional star appearing through the branches and the scent of cedar thick in the air, the owls seemed a greater mystery than the inheritance.

"I've only seen them on TV before. Don't fly away before I'm finished,"Gina whispered, half to herself and half to the birds.

By the time the sketches were complete, Nicole's eyes were drooping again. "I know we have to beat Tyler to the answers, but I can't handle looking at the will right now," she complained. "My brain has shut down for the night."

Sue and Gina nodded, yawning. They agreed to try again first thing in the morning.

• • •

In the morning, however, Rose had other plans. It seemed like the sun had barely risen when she knocked on the bedroom door. "Get up, lazy bones!" she called. "There's a surfing instructor meeting you at the beach in an hour."

Sue was immediately wide awake. "Surfing? I'm in. Where did I put my board? Is there stuff for breakfast? Come on—everybody up!"

Within an hour, they were introducing themselves to their instructor—Donna—at Long Beach. Donna was long and lean, with muscles in her arms that looked like tightly woven cords. She seemed tough and scanned them with a careful eye as they pulled on matching black wetsuits, shivering in the damp breeze.

"This looks seriously unsafe," Gina worried, gazing at the plumes of white spray hitting the rocks at the edge of the bay. As they watched, a wetsuit-clad figure leapt to his feet, cutting across one of the waves. The water seemed to be chasing him, tearing closer and closer until finally it toppled him in a wall of foam. Gina held her breath until she saw his head pop to the surface a moment later.

"It can be dangerous," Donna nodded, "but when you're a born-and-bred Tofino girl, this looks like your backyard."

"A backyard with sharks," Gina muttered.

Donna gave what could have been a smile. "No need to worry about sharks. There are strong currents, though. No one wants to go near those rocks. We're going to stay fairly shallow, in the middle of the bay. We'll swim out together."

The temperature wasn't too bad, thanks to the wetsuits, but the waves looked even bigger than they had from the beach. Donna straddled her surfboard effortlessly, looking completely comfortable. She was surprisingly encouraging.

"You're doing great!" she called to the girls.

Gina felt more like a piece of driftwood getting tossed around. "We're all likely to drown," she grumbled to herself, but she continued to paddle further from the shore.

Sue had surfed before, so it was only a few minutes before she was riding a cresting wave toward the beach. Gina and Nicole found it more difficult to balance. They lay atop their boards, waiting as Donna watched the waves.

"Here's one—go! Paddle with your arms. Now up on your knees—"

Crash! Within seconds, Gina toppled from the board into the water. She surfaced spluttering to find Nicole doing the same nearby.

Then, after two more falls, she finally "caught" her first wave. She paddled hard at Donna's cue and, just as she was rising to her knees, she felt the wave swell under her board and propel her forward. Then she was up and sweeping toward the shore as if there were a sail attached to her.

At the end of the lesson, the girls staggered exhausted onto the sand and eagerly clutched the mugs of hot chocolate Donna filled from her Thermos.

PRESSURE

Ever wonder how those huge, heavy ships actually float? And what allows submarines to go up and down in the water? Pressure is an important principle for buoyancy and lift; it helps explain why heavy ships can float and submarines can submerge. Pressure also helps partly explain why it is much harder to surf standing up than lying down on a surfboard.

Pressure is described as a force exerted on a certain area. The equation reads:

$$P = \frac{F}{A}$$

where P = pressure, F = force, and A = area. An object weighing very little can exert a great amount of pressure if the force acts only on a very small surface area. On the other hand, an object weighing a lot can exert little pressure if the force acts on a large surface area. For example, if you put the pointed end of a nail on a piece of wood and then a brick on the nail, the weight of the brick will exert a lot of pressure through the small, pointy surface area of the nail and probably will put a puncture mark on the piece of wood. However, if you take that same brick and lay it on the piece of wood, it will not damage the wood. You could even double the weight by adding a second brick and you will not damage the piece of wood because the *pressure* of the bricks is exerting *force* on a large surface area of the wood.

This is why firefighters or police officers, when trying to rescue someone who has fallen through thin ice, will lie on their stomachs to reach the person rather than walk out onto the ice in an upright position. When they are lying on their stomachs, they are distributing their body weight over a much larger surface area and are therefore exerting less pressure than they would be if they were standing upright (where their body weight would be exerting much more pressure through the smaller surface area of their feet). It's the same when Gina and Nicole lie on their surfboards. They are distributing more of their body weight on the surfboards and they won't sink. However, when they try to stand on the boards, their weight is exerting much more pressure through the smaller surface area of their feet. If they have small surfboards, they will start sinking a bit, unless they catch a good wave to give their boards lift. (Of course, they also have to learn to balance on their boards so they won't fall off!)

"You did great!" she said. The cold had flushed her cheeks and her excitement made her seem less intimidating.

Gina turned to look at the water. "I still can't believe I actually surfed!" Suddenly, she saw something—no, someone!—far out in the bay. She squinted to be sure, not wanting to make a fool of herself in front of Donna. It was definitely a person.

"Someone's out there! He's waving his arms like he's in trouble."

Donna spun quickly into action. She told the girls to stay where they were, then she called to another group of surfers resting on the sand. "Someone's in trouble!" Two sprinted toward the beach, while a third ran toward his pack and grabbed a cellphone.

Gina, Sue, and Nicole watched as Donna and the other surfers flung themselves onto their boards and paddled hard, their strong arms churning through the waves. It seemed like only a couple of minutes before they'd grabbed the person in trouble. The three bobbed together in the waves for a while, then the mystery figure threw his arms across one of the boards and the surfers propelled themselves back to shore.

As they reached the sand and released their grips on the drowning man, the three girls ran to join them. "Is he okay? That was amazing—I can't believe how fast you guys got out there!" said Sue.

Donna gave them a tired smile. "He must have got caught in a current. He was too tired to swim back. I think he'll be fine now."

"An ambulance is on its way," said the surfer with the cellphone, joining them.

"Rip tide," the half-drowned man sputtered, slowly pushing himself off the sand. Unlike the other people in the bay, this man seemed more equipped for swimming than for surfing. He was wearing black flippers and a snorkel. "I'm okay now."

As he pulled off his mask, Sue was the first to recognize him. "Tyler!"

Gina looked at Sue and raised her eyebrows. "I guess all that surfer lingo didn't help him float. A real surfer would have known more about the currents out there."

Sue nodded. "He looks more like a drowned rat than a surfer to me." ✱

PRESSURE EXPERIMENT

Materials:
- ✱ an empty, clear plastic bottle (about 500 mL size) used for water, juice, or pop
- ✱ a knitting needle (1 mm thickness) or skewer to puncture the bottle
- ✱ a felt marker
- ✱ a tape measure

Procedure:
1. Remove the paper label from the bottle.
2. Measure with the tape measure from the opening of the bottle down its length and draw a dot with the marker at 4 cm, 8 cm and 12 cm from the bottle opening.
3. Carefully use the knitting needle or thin skewer to poke little holes through the bottle where you drew the dots.
4. Place the bottle in the sink and fill it to the top with tap water.
5. Observe the three jets of water and the distances they travel as the bottle empties.

What Happened?

Remember that the greater the force on a given area, the greater the pressure. At the top of the bottle, there are fewer water molecules pushing down to where the first hole is located, so there is less weight and force acting on the water. Therefore, with little pressure being exerted on the water flowing out of the top hole, that stream of water is the closest distance to the bottle. At the second hole, more weight of water and more pressure are being exerted so the water travels a farther distance from the bottle. The bottom hole has the greatest weight of water pushing down on it and thus the greatest amount of pressure. This stream of water is the farthest away from the bottle. Also notice that as the level of the water decreases, the pressure on the streams of water also decreases and the distance the water flows from the bottle decreases. Eventually the water from the top hole and then the middle and lowest holes end up trickling down the side of the bottle.

6

Chart-ing the Course

Rose wasn't home when the girls returned from their surfing lesson, so they gathered in the living room with three fresh hot chocolates. Sue and Nicole got out the will and leaned over the pages. They were working from a photocopy—Rose had rushed the original to her lawyer.

Gina, still chilled from the waves, decided to light a fire.

"Maybe we're looking at it upside down," Nicole suggested, taking the rectangular chart and turning it the other way.

"That doesn't help me," Sue complained, coughing a few times.

"What are our possibilities?" Nicole asked, mostly to herself. "It looks like some sort of a grid, a chart, a graph...." A whiff of smoke hit her nose and she coughed through the rest of her sentence.

"What's going on? Gina! You're—"

"You're smoking us out!" Sue finished the sentence, getting up to fling open the door and the windows.

Gina's eyes were already watering from the smoke. "I don't get why it's not working. Rose used it yesterday."

"Did you open the damper?" Sue asked. Gina stared at her blankly.

Sighing, Sue headed for the fireplace and flipped the damper lever forward. "When you light the fire, you have to open the damper so the chimney can suck up the smoke. Once it's burning well, you can close the damper a bit to hold in the heat."

"Alright, so I guess I wasn't a girl guide. You don't have to be bossy about it," Gina snapped. Then she looked slightly apologetic.

"Now that it's lit, can we close the windows again and concentrate on the will?"

Together, they turned back to the pages, but Nicole was gone. They found her in front of the computer. "Wait a second," she said. "I think I've almost got it."

Sue hated to wait. "You think you've almost got what? Do you know what the chart is?"

"I might," Nicole said slowly, waiting for an image to download. "I think it might be... There!"

She was right. The outlines of the chart on the screen matched the one in the will. "Hey!" Gina said, peering over Nicole's shoulder. "That's the Periodic Table. We studied that in science this year."

"But what does it have to do with Rose's uncle?" Nicole wondered, her forehead creasing.

Sue held up the page of the will beside the screen. "Don't forget the shaded boxes. What elements are they?"

Counting the squares, Nicole found both of them. "Hydrogen and oxygen."

"H_2O!" Gina said immediately. "The chemical formula for

68

water. That's what Tyler was doing in the ocean. It's obvious—the inheritance is underwater!" She scrambled for the next page of the will—the map—and pointed to the shoreline at the edge. "Maybe this is Chesterman Beach."

Sue and Nicole gazed at her, then at the chart, wondering if she could be right. Then Nicole slowly shook her head. "I don't think so," she said. "For one thing, there's no '2' on the chart. H and O don't equal water."

"And Rose's uncle couldn't swim," Sue said. "Remember she told us that, when she was talking about his smuggling?"

Gina was silent, unwilling to admit that they were right.

"What else could H and O mean? It could be initials," Nicole said.

"It could be Ho Ho Ho," Sue suggested.

Gina rolled her eyes. "I think we can safely assume it doesn't refer to Santa. This map may not show Chesterman Beach, but it doesn't show the North Pole, either."

The girls fell silent, each thinking hard. Sue played idly with the map while she thought, tracing the topographic lines with her finger, then tracing the horizontal and vertical lines. Suddenly, she stopped. Her finger was resting on the letter H.

"They're coordinates," she said quietly. "We should have figured it out right away."

"They're what?" Nicole asked. She and Gina moved closer.

"Look," Sue pointed to the shoreline on the map. "Let's say this is Chesterman Beach. That would put our cabin here." She jabbed a fingernail toward the high ground at the end of a black line.

"That could be our driveway," Gina agreed.

"Now look at the letters along the top and the side. The ones at the top go from A to L, and the ones along the side go from M to Z, right?"

ATOMS

Why did Gina say that water was "H_2O"? Gina knew that matter is made up of molecules and molecules are made up of small particles called atoms. Atoms are very, very small and are the building blocks of matter. Because atoms are so small, they cannot be weighed on a scale. The atomic mass unit (amu) is a special unit to measure the mass of an atom and its particles.

The centre of an atom is called a nucleus and is made up of protons and neutrons. Atoms also have electrons that orbit around the nucleus. Protons have a positive (+) charge, meaning that a proton is a positive particle. The electron is a negative particle, meaning it has a negative (–) charge. A neutron has no charge and is a neutral particle. Atoms are normally electrically neutral because they usually have the same number of protons (positive charges) as electrons (negative charges). So they balance each other out. Two common atoms are oxygen and hydrogen. In fact, water is made up of two hydrogen atoms and one oxygen atom, which is why Gina said the chemical formula for water is H_2O.

For more information:

http://science.howstuffworks.com/atom1.htm

http://www.nyu.edu/pages/mathmol/textbook/ atoms.html

http://www.shu.ac.uk/pri/scripts/resources/uploaded/ atoms_main.htm

http://school.discovery.com/sciencefaircentral/ jakesattic/lab/electricity.html

Gina and Nicole both nodded.

"Now follow the H line and the O line to where they intersect." Marking her place, Sue felt on the floor with her other hand until she found a pencil. She carefully marked an X at the coordinates.

"The X is only a few kilometres away," she finished.

Nicole took the map and examined it again. "It looks like we take the trail toward the tree platform and keep going. But it goes from a dashed line to a dotted line—that could mean the trail disappears."

Sue smirked at her. "You're not scared, are you? After all, didn't you just win the award for best orienteering?"

"Is that a challenge?" Nicole smiled back.

"Wait. It's five o'clock. It's almost dinnertime, and Rose is going to be back soon," Gina protested, but no one listened. Forgetting her sore muscles from the surfing lesson, Sue had already laced her boots and was standing impatiently by the door while Nicole gathered her things.

"We have to at least leave a note for Rose," Gina said in her most responsible voice.

"Are you kidding? She'll think we've lost our minds again," Sue told her. "If you hurry up, we'll be back before she gets home."

"I'll just tell her we've gone for a walk," Gina compromised, scribbling quickly.

Nicole grabbed the compass and shoved it in a pocket of her rain jacket. With the map in hand, she led the other two out the door.

Within a few minutes, they were hiking past the tree platform and into the forest. ✦

ELEMENTS

 Gina recognized the chart as the Periodic Table, which lists and classifies all known elements. An element is the simplest type of matter that cannot be split into a simpler substance. Elements are made up of only one kind of atom. There are more than 100 elements. Most elements are found in nature and the others are created in laboratories. The atoms of each element have a specific number of protons and neutrons in the nucleus and a specific number of electrons orbiting around the nucleus. All atoms of the same element are all exactly the same. All elements are labelled by one or two letters, often a short form of the Latin name of the element. For example, hydrogen is labelled "H" and oxygen is "O." Scientists have classified elements into two broad categories: metals and non-metals. Metals include gold (Au), silver (Ag), copper (Cu), and iron (Fe). Non-metals include gases like helium (He) and oxygen (O) or brittle solids like sulphur (S) and carbon (C). Elements can combine with other elements to form new substances. These new substances are called compounds. Water, for example, is a compound because it is made up of hydrogen (H) and oxygen (O). Table salt is another example. It is made up of sodium (Na) and chlorine (Cl), which forms sodium chloride.

The Periodic Table gives basic information about all known elements. The information in the Periodic Table includes the element's name, its atomic mass, and its atomic number. The atomic mass is measured by atomic mass units (see p. 70).The atomic number is the number of protons in the nucleus, and each element has a different atomic number. The Periodic Table is arranged in rows from smallest to largest atomic number. It is also arranged in columns according to how the element behaves when forming compounds. Elements are also grouped and colour-coded in the Periodic Table by classes of elements, such as various types of gases, metals, non-metals and so on. The Periodic Table is very useful for scientists. For example, a scientist can use gold's atomic mass to calculate how many gold atoms there are in a one-kilogram block of gold.

For more information:

http://www.chem4kids.com/files/elem_intro.html
http://education.jlab.org/elementflashcards/index.html
http://pearl1.lanl.gov/periodic/default.htm

CHEMICAL REACTIONS

 Sue may not have realized that she was creating a chemical reaction with her fire. Chemical reactions are exchanges of electrons or changes in the sharing of electrons between atoms. The electron is the most interesting part of the atom. Each element has a specific number of electrons in each of its atoms. The number of electrons determines the chemical properties of an atom. Chemical properties determine how elements act during chemical reactions. Unlike physical properties of an element, which can be determined by our senses (you can see colour, feel texture, etc.), chemical properties of elements cannot be identified by our senses alone. Chemical properties are determined through different types of chemical analyses. Chemical reactions occur when the chemical properties of the substances change to create new substances. Iron rusting and milk going sour are examples of chemical reactions.

Sue's fire is also a chemical reaction. Fire comes about from a chemical reaction between the oxygen in the room and the wood in the fireplace, which would have been heated with kindling and a match. When the wood reaches about 150 degrees Celsius, it decomposes (breaks down) into smoke, char, and ash. The smoke is made up of compounds of hydrogen, oxygen, and carbon. The char is almost pure carbon (and is what you buy when you get charcoal for your barbecue). The ash is composed of all the unburned elements left in the wood. When the gases get hot enough, the compounds break up and the atoms of hydrogen, oxygen, and carbon recombine to form water, carbon dioxide, carbon monoxide, and other chemicals. The side effect of this chemical reaction is heat.

For more information:

http://www.howstuffworks.com/fire1.html

http://www.angliacampus.com/education/fire/secondarl/ fire.htm

CHEMICAL REACTIONS EXPERIMENT

Be sure you check with an adult before you begin this or any other experiment that might be dangerous!

Materials:
* a candle
* a candlestick holder
* matches
* a spoon
* facial tissues

Procedure:

1. Place the candle in the candlestick holder.
2. Carefully light the candle with the matches.
3. Observe the candle burning over a two-minute period.
4. Holding the spoon by the handle, place the bowl of the spoon just above the candle flame for three seconds (count to three) and remove.
5. Let the spoon cool for about three minutes, *as it will be very hot*. Then observe the coating on the spoon and wipe with the tissue.
6. Blow out the candle and observe the smoke.

What Happened?

A candle is composed of paraffin wax. Paraffin is a hydrocarbon because it is made up of long, complicated chainlike molecules of carbon (C) and hydrogen (H) atoms. When the wick is lit by the match, the wax around the candle flame is heated. The heat causes the long chainlike molecules to untangle and break up, turning the wax from a solid into a thin liquid. As the liquid wax nears the flame, the heat from the flame causes the wax to turn into vapour and mix with the oxygen. These vapours are drawn into the flame where they ignite and produce the light and heat of the candle.

The burning process causes the liquid wax and oxygen to break down into a mixture of gases, water vapour, and small solid particles. The gases produced when the carbon (C) from the candle wax mixes with the oxygen (O) are mostly carbon dioxide (CO_2) and carbon monoxide (CO). The small solid particles (or soot) are mostly unburned carbon (C). Carbon is the black stuff that you scrape off a piece of burnt toast. It is also the black stuff that you wiped off the spoon with the tissue. As long as the flame is not disturbed, the carbon burns up inside the flame. When you put the spoon over the flame, it causes a disturbance in the flame, which allows some of the carbon to escape before it burns up. These tiny bits of carbon rise from the flame to form the smoke that you see. But not all smoke is made up of bits of carbon. When you blew out your candle, the smoke would have been white, not black as you saw earlier. This smoke is made of tiny bits of wax that have not come apart yet, so there is no visible carbon. That is why the smoke is white instead of black.

7

Lost and Found

Winding its way around giant cedars, the trail continued uphill from the tree platform. Sue and Nicole led while Gina lagged behind, still unhappy that she had been overruled.

"It wouldn't have killed us to wait until tomorrow," she muttered.

Not paying attention, she almost ran into Nicole's back.

"See how these two trails intersect on the map?" Nicole was saying. "I think if we turn south here, we'll get to the X faster."

"Two trails intersect?" Gina looked around and finally noticed a rough path to one side. "That's what you call a trail?"

"A game trail, probably," Nicole answered as she started down it.

"Game trail. Great. Would that be game as in cougars? Bears? Yes, let's walk down it. That sounds like a great idea."

Sue glanced back, smirking. "Your sarcasm isn't actually help-ing, Gina."

"Ouch!"

"What now?" Sue and Nicole turned to look, but Gina waved them forward.

"Keep going, at least a few more steps."

The girls did as instructed, then stopped again. "What is it?"

"A wasp stung me! You two walked over a nest and stirred it up. When I walked through, they got revenge."

It was obviously hurting, but the sting didn't look too serious. The group turned east once more, checking their heading more often on the compass as the trail began to fade away. In another twenty minutes, all three were sore. Nicole was limping slightly as if she had blisters starting, and Sue had had a nasty run-in with some stinging nettles.

"We've got to be almost there," Gina said.

"Almost," Nicole answered calmly, checking the map. "Can you hear that stream? That's our last landmark."

In a few more minutes, the girls had pushed their way out of the underbrush and they were standing on the banks of a creek.

"Did you call this a landmark?" Gina asked. "Looks more like an obstacle to me."

But Nicole was determined. "A minor obstacle. See that tree trunk? We can shimmy across it to the other side."

The trunk she pointed to was over a metre above the creek, and the water below looked cold and fast.

"You can't be serious," Gina said. But Nicole was already scampering to the other side.

Taking a deep breath and steeling herself not to look down, she crawled across the log. It wasn't as bad as she had expected, although it hurt the wasp sting on her calf. She kept an eye on Sue's

WASPS

Getting stung by a wasp is no fun. Gina got stung because Sue and Nicole disturbed the wasp's nest. Wasps will always defend their nests. The most common wasp is a yellowjacket. Yellowjackets can be aerial nesters (above ground) or ground nesters. A fertilized queen finds a nesting site in the spring and begins her nest with a small "comb" of about a dozen cells (little compartments) enclosed by wood-fibre paper. She makes this paper by chewing wood or plant fibres mixed with water. The nest starts about the size of a golfball, and the queen lays and deposits an egg in each cell that she looks after herself. The eggs develop into larvae (wingless immature forms of many insects). Next the larvae spin silk caps to close off their cells and become pupae (a resting stage in which the larval structure changes to an adult).

They then shed their pupal skins, chew through their silk cell cap, and emerge as adult daughters to the queen. These daughters become workers to the queen. The queen lays more eggs while the workers help feed the larvae and make the nest bigger. Later in the season, some of these larvae become males and others become next year's queens. Only the queens live over the winter; the other wasps die.

Wasps are carnivores. They eat aphids, caterpillars, insect larvae, and almost anything that preys on gardens and crops. So they are beneficial for the ecosystem and to farmers. They also need carbohydrates, including sugar. They will feed on nectar, fruits, and your picnic.

Wasps, unlike bees, can sting many times. A bee's stinger has larger barbs (little hooks) along the edge of the stinger. After stinging someone, the bee is unable to pull the stinger out of the wound of the person it strung. When the bee tries to fly away, the stinger pulls away from its abdomen and the bee dies. The wasp, on the other hand, has very small barbs, more like the jagged edges of a steak knife. So a wasp can pull its stinger out of the wound and fly away.

For more information:

http://cybersleuthkids.com/sleuth/Science/Animals/Insects/ Wasps/

http://www.bugbios.com/entophiles/hymenoptera/

http://www.winnipeg-bugline.com/bee.html

feet ahead of her, and she was across the water before she had time to get scared.

Once on the opposite bank, Nicole seemed to run out of ideas. "We're standing right where the X is on the map," she said, looking around blankly. "But I don't see anything. Do you think we have to dig or something?"

Nicole handed Gina the map and compass and started scanning the ground for anything unusual. Sue quickly joined her. Gina sighed and leaned against a tree. She stretched her sore legs, rolled her shoulders a few times, then tilted her neck from one side to the other. Suddenly, something in the branches caught her eye. It was a piece of flagging tape, and, when she walked closer to investigate, she found a small knothole in the tree trunk.

"I think I've got something," she called.

Nicole and Sue were immediately beside her, and they watched as Gina reached into the knothole. "I feel something. Let me see if I can grab it."

Slowly, she pulled her hand out and peeled back her fingers to reveal a tiny wooden box. "Look! It has Rose's name on it!"

The box was only a few centimetres across, but it was intricately carved. Tiny leaves and flowers wrapped around the chiselled letters R-O-S-E.

"Open it! Open it!" Sue reached for the box impatiently and lifted the lid. Or tried to. She could see where the box was meant to open, but it wouldn't budge.

"Let me try," Gina said, taking the box back. Wiggling one of her fingernails into the gap in the wood, she tried to pry the lid off.

"It's not working," she admitted finally. " And I don't want to break it."

"Let's take it to the cabin and try there," Nicole suggested. " We should start back soon anyway."

Nodding, Gina slipped the box into one of her jacket pockets and tucked Nicole's compass in the other.

This time Nicole and Sue were more confident on the log bridge, scampering quickly across. Gina followed on her hands and knees, telling herself not to look down. Suddenly a wasp buzzed by her ear. Gina swatted at it. Her other hand lost its grip on the damp bark and for a second she was sliding toward the water. She heard Sue yelp from the bank.

"Hang on!"

Frantically, Gina threw her arms around the log and stopped her fall. "I'm okay," she called. Sue was already with her, though, holding her shoulders for balance as she wiggled around to the top of the log. With Sue sliding slowly backwards and Gina shakily following, they made it to the other side.

"Thanks," she breathed to Sue, standing to brush herself off.

Nicole hugged her quickly. "I'm glad you're okay. Now, should I get us out of here? Rose is probably home by now."

Gina nodded and reached into her pocket for the compass. Then, with a sick feeling in her stomach, she looked up at Nicole. "I don't have the compass. I put it in my pocket. It must have slipped out when I fell."

"Do you still have the box?" Sue asked. Gina checked her other pocket and nodded with relief.

"Still here."

"But now how do we get home?" Sue asked.

Nicole was still calm and logical. "I know two ways to find north without a compass. First, moss grows on the north side of trees."

"Is that true?" Sue asked. "I thought that only worked in movies."

"I think it's true," Nicole said. "The other way is to point the hour hand of my watch at the sun. The line between the hour hand and the minute hand should point north."

SORE MUSCLES

Sue's muscles were sore from surfing. What caused her muscles to get sore? Exercise can cause two types of muscle soreness. The first type is the muscle soreness you feel during, or right after, exercise. It is called immediate muscle soreness. The second type occurs 24 to 48 hours after the exercise and disappears after about 72 hours. It is called delayed-onset muscle soreness (DOMS). It occurs in people who are doing a new activity they haven't done before or in people who are exercising longer and harder than they have done in the past. Because Sue felt her soreness the next day, she was suffering from DOMS. There are many theories and controversies about what causes DOMS. Different theories have suggested that muscle soreness is due to lactic acid buildup or muscle growth. The most current research suggests that DOMS is caused by tiny injuries primarily to tendons (the tough and inelastic fibrous tissue that connects muscles to other body parts, like bones) and ligaments (the tough and fibrous tissue that connects bones or cartilage at your joints).

How can Sue get rid of her muscle soreness? Many studies have researched various treatments for muscle soreness, including creams and medications, massaging, stretching, and the application of ice to the sore muscle (called cryotherapy). So far, however, none of these methods have proved to be useful in reducing DOMS, although some of the treatments can help a bit if they are used right away after intense or unusual exercise. The good news for Sue is that once she has experienced DOMS at that specific level of exercise intensity, she shouldn't experience that soreness again unless she increases the intensity or does some totally different activity. This is because muscles quickly adapt to exercise intensity during regular exercise programs. So, unless Sue decides to go surfing for an even longer and more intense time, her muscle soreness should not reoccur.

For more information:

http://www.acefitness.org/fitfacts/
fitfacts_display.cfm?itemid=55

Gina looked at Sue and nodded. "I knew we brought her along for a reason."

The methods seemed to work, but the girls could only move slowly through the underbrush. Before long, the sun was sinking out of sight behind the trees and the forest quickly grew dark. Nicole led them north for as long as she could, but finally she turned to face them. With the canopy of branches blocking any last evening light, it was hard even to see her face clearly.

"We can't go any farther," she told them, trying to keep her voice steady. "We'll just get more lost. I think we're going to have to stay here and wait. Rose will come and find us, or we'll find our way back in the morning."

"This wouldn't…" Gina fell quiet. She was going to say that this wouldn't have happened if they had listened to her about leaving so late in the day. Then she remembered that it was her fault they were lost.

The girls found a sheltered spot where low branches had kept the forest floor dry, and they sat close together. It grew darker until they could only see the closest trees. Soon they could barely see each other. The night grew louder as the wind picked up and each sound seemed magnified by the darkness. The girls huddled in silence, as if wishing they were invisible.

It seemed like hours later when they suddenly heard the loud snap of wood nearby and a crash of leaves and branches. ✦

WATCH-AS-COMPASS EXPERIMENT

How did Nicole use her watch as a compass? Try this yourself.

Materials:

✳ a working watch with hands

✳ sunshine (the experiment is more complicated on cloudy days)

Procedure:

1. Stand in a sunny place outdoors.
2. Hold the face of the watch in the palm of your hand.
3. Turn it so the hour hand of the watch is pointing toward the sun. *(Be careful not to look directly into the sun.)*
4. Take the midway point between the hour hand and 12 o'clock; that's the direction of south (see diagram).
5. Draw an imaginary diagonal line from this point through the centre of the clock face. The opposite side would be facing north.
6. Once you know where south and north are, you can determine where east and west are by drawing imaginary diagonals in the shape of a cross (see diagram on page 88).

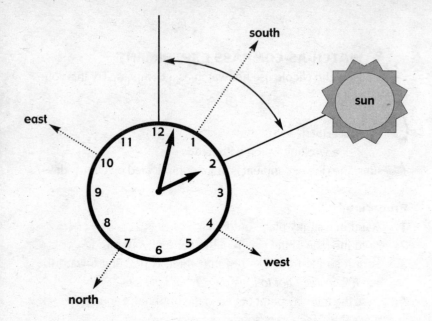

What Happened

Every day, the sun rises in the east and sets in the west. It completes a 24-hour cycle, making a full rotation so that the sun is in the same place at 12 noon each day. In the northern hemisphere at 12 noon, the sun sits south. So, if you point the hour hand toward the sun at 12 noon, you would be facing south. Before 12 noon, if you point the hour hand toward the sun, the sun would lie counter-clockwise (moving left around the face of the clock) from 12 o'clock. After 12 noon, the sun would lie clockwise (moving right around the face of the clock) from 12 o'clock. During the 24-hour day, even though the earth made one rotation, the hour hand goes around the face of your watch two times. So the distance the hour hand travels and its angle must be divided in half.

For more information:

http://www.time4watches.com/Watch%20Articles/
  using_a_watch_as_a_compass.htm

8

Trash or Treasure?

"I thought we were going to be there all night," Sue wailed into the shoulder of Rose's jacket. Rose was holding her in a tight bear hug and lecturing her at the same time.

"You girls should have known better than to traipse off into the forest that late in the day." The girls were gathered at the front door of the cabin, where a search and rescue volunteer had just delivered them. The glow from the fireplace inside looked more welcoming than ever before.

"I can't believe that a dog helped find us! We're lucky you know that search and rescue guy." Nicole tried to sound calm, but she was shivering and wiping away the remains of a few tears at the same time.

"I have never been so happy to hear a dog bark in my entire life," Gina echoed.

Suddenly Sue remembered the results of their hike and extracted herself from Rose's arms. "Gina, show Rose the box that we found," she said.

They were interrupted by headlights coming up the driveway When the car rolled to a stop, Tyler stepped out. "Sorry I didn't carve in earlier, babe," he said to Rose. "I just got your message. But I see it's all primo now."

"Ugh. If he had tried to rescue us, I would have run farther into the forest," Sue muttered, but only Nicole was close enough to hear her.

Rose shepherded the group inside and soon had them settled in the living room with blankets and cups of tea. "There, I've got everyone safely home. I can't imagine what I would have said to your mothers…"

Rose's voice trailed off and she fixed Sue with a quizzical look. "Sue, weren't you saying something about showing me a box you'd found? Is that why you girls were out on the trail so late in the day? You didn't just go for a walk. It has something to do with this crazy will, doesn't it?"

Sue looked toward Tyler cautiously. He'd been sprawled on the sofa but now he stiffened, and Sue imagined that she could actually see his ears snapping to attention. When she looked away, she caught Nicole's eye.

"It may be something you want to look at in private," Nicole suggested.

"If it's important enough to drag you through the forest at night, it's important enough for me to see now. Out with it."

Gina slowly drew the box out of her pocket and handed it to Rose, casting a sidelong glance at Tyler. His eyes were riveted on the box.

"You think he made this for me?" Rose asked in amazement.

When the girls nodded, she tried to pry off the lid.

"We couldn't open it, either," Gina told her, yawning. Nicole and Sue echoed her yawn before they could stop themselves. Without further discussion, Rose placed the box on the hearth and herded them all toward bed.

• • •

The morning was sunny and warm, and the group lazed around the cabin. Sue was industriously attacking the breakfast dishes, and Nicole had curled up on the couch with her book. Gina had spread newspapers on the floor near the door to the porch and she had her hands buried in a basin of mud. Having decided that she was probably bit by a yellowjacket, she was apparently trying to construct a model of a wasp's nest.

"Hey, I thought I was the naturalist of this bunch. Why the sudden interest?" Sue asked.

Gina glanced up from her project, looking slightly sheepish. "I think it's the rain forest. It seems like there are unusual creatures everywhere we go. Is it illegal to have a new interest?"

"Maybe we'll both turn into biologists after all," Sue grinned.

"That's going to take hours," Nicole said, nodding toward the nest-in-progress.

Gina shrugged, unconcerned. "Do you have somewhere to go?"

Rose, meanwhile, was wandering slowly through the room, tidying stacks of magazines and collecting random dishes. When she reached the hearth, she picked up the carved box.

At her gasp, the girls were instantly alert.

"What's going on?" Sue asked, leaning over the counter from the kitchen.

"It opened." When Rose turned toward them, they could see she had removed the lid. She reached inside and slowly pulled out something that sparkled.

"What is it?" Gina asked, hurrying over. She reached for it, then looked at the mud on her hands and stopped.

"It looks like a crystal," Rose answered, examining it. It was attached to a thin string of fishing line.

"How did you get the box open?"

"I just lifted off the lid," Rose said.

"Maybe it was damp," Nicole suggested, taking the box and turning it in her small hands. "The wood might have swollen. When the box sat by the fireplace all night, the heat dried it out."

"What do we do next?" Sue asked.

Rose smiled at her enthusiasm. "Why don't we all bike into town, and we can ask the jeweller. Maybe there's something special about this crystal."

The girls scrambled to get ready. "Bring your camera," Rose told Sue.

• • •

The jeweller was a tall, thin man with a wizened face. He nodded patiently as the girls tumbled through the story of the will and the crystal. Then he tucked a magnifying glass against his eye and leaned down to examine the bauble.

"Well? What do you think?" Sue was too impatient to wait for the jeweller to finish his inspection.

"It's certainly lovely," he said, straightening.

"But is it valuable?" Sue asked.

"I'm afraid not," he told her. "It's a beautiful prism, but it's merely decorative. You could probably buy one down the street at the gift shop for four or five dollars."

Sue wilted with disappointment, but Rose didn't seem surprised at all by the news. She thanked the jeweller. "Maybe I can wear the prism as a necklace," she said as she ushered the girls outside.

"Who else can we ask?" Nicole wondered. "Maybe we need a second opinion."

"Not just now, I don't think," Rose said, checking her watch. "We're due at the docks." She refused to answer any more questions until the three girls were standing beside a large Zodiac boat, tugging on orange survival suits.

DRIFTWOOD

 Everyone has seen driftwood before, but just what is it? Driftwood is generally found on the shores of bodies of water, such as oceans and lakes. Driftwood may consist of entire uprooted trees, roots of logged or dead trees, or any parts of trees or shrubs that have been washed into the seas in storms or due to erosion. In the Arctic, where there are no trees as we know them in the south, driftwood was often the only source of wood for fuel or toolmaking for the Inuit. They would gather pieces of driftwood and strap them together with hide or sinews to fashion runners for sleds and frames for kayaks. They also used driftwood to make tools and sometimes lived in houses made from driftwood and sod.

For more information:

**http://cgdi.gc.ca/ccatlas/joamie/humgeog/culture/
  culture.htm**
**http://www.civilization.ca/educat/oracle/modules/
  dmorrison/page01_e.html**

SURVIVAL SUITS

Sue, Nicole, and Gina put on survival suits before they got into the Zodiac. In many parts of the world, survival suits are standard equipment on ships, fishing vessels, offshore oil rigs, and other ocean platforms. They are also used during offshore helicopter flights. Survival suits help people survive if they go overboard in cold water by preventing the rapid onset of hypothermia. Hypothermia occurs when a person's body temperature drops because of exposure to cold. These virtually waterproof suits provide flotation and insulation to protect people from the cold water and icy winds. They are also equipped with emergency beacons that feature flashing lights, which help rescuers in their search.

The suits work by using materials that are poor conductors of heat. On p. 152 of *Science Squad #1*, we learned that whenever there is a temperature difference, heat energy is transferred from the hotter place to the cooler place until the temperature achieves thermal equilibrium (becomes the same). This means that if a person is in water that is 10 degrees Celsius, the person's normal body temperature of 37 degrees Celsius would eventually drop to 10 degrees Celsius. Survivals suits work by insulating the body so that the heat energy of the person's body does not transfer to the cold water so quickly.

Without these suits, a person can lose consciousness within one hour in water colder than 10 degrees Celsius.

What makes good insulators and poor insulators goes right back to atoms and electrons (see p. 70). Electrons that have escaped from the orbits of their atom are called free electrons. These free electrons can easily move from atom to atom. Many materials, like metals, have free electrons, and they are good heat conductors because they can transfer energy quickly through their free electrons moving from atom to atom. Other materials do not allow electrons to flow easily and these materials are poor conductors. Poor conductors are also called insulators.

To make a good survival suit, you must make it from good insulators. Because survival suits are designed for cold water, the suits must be tested to see how well they insulate heat before they can be approved. The manufacture and approval of survival suits should be regulated by something called an "immersion suit standard."

For more information:

http://www.stemnet.nf.ca/CITE/shuttleliving.htm
http://tea.rice.edu/carvellas/7.17.2002.html

"This is Hazel," Rose said, introducing them to a strong-looking guide dressed in a similar survival suit. "I've got to work this afternoon, but Hazel's going to introduce you to some of my favourite neighbours."

Within a few minutes, Rose was waving from the dock as the girls and Hazel bumped across the waves, the Zodiac's motor rumbling loudly and the wind whipping their cheeks. "We should be there in about twenty minutes," Hazel yelled above the wind. "They're close today."

Rose's neighbours turned out to be whales. Huge, truck-sized whales, rubbing themselves against the rocky shore and sending sudden spouts of water into the air. Sue was frantically snapping pictures.

"These are grey whales," Hazel told them. "They're known scientifically as baleen whales, because they eat by straining the ocean water through baleen in their mouths. That lets them collect tiny fish, shrimp, and squid."

"What's baleen?" Sue asked from behind her camera.

"It's what these whales have instead of teeth. It's make of a material similar to your fingernails, and the whales have huge plates of it."

"And why are they rubbing themselves on the rocks?"

"It helps dislodge the barnacles that attach themselves to the whales."

Their questions answered, the girls were content to bob quietly in the boat for more than half an hour, watching the whales jostle against one another in the shallow water. When Hazel finally turned the boat toward home, the warm sun had made everyone sleepy. Gina and Nicole soon closed their eyes and nestled into the protection of their survival suits.

Curled into her seat, Sue watched the bow of the boat through half-open lids. With each wave, an arc of spray splashed into the air. As Hazel pulled the boat in a gentle curve to avoid a piece of driftwood, the sun shone through the spray. The light passed through the water droplets and sent tiny rainbows flying over the sides of the boat.

Sue sat up, suddenly wide awake. Those rainbows had given her an idea. ✦

GREY WHALES

Gina, Sue, and Nicole are enjoying their whale watching along the coast of British Columbia. Grey whales like to spend their summers feeding in the Gulf of Alaska and the Bering Sea. In the winter they migrate south, travelling from the Bering Sea to the coast of southern California. They travel back and forth by following the west coast of North America. They find their way by using landmarks and following two easy rules. In the autumn, they travel by keeping the land to the left of them. In the spring, they do the reverse; they keep the land to their right. This method of orienting is called piloting.

Whales are mammals that left their life on land many thousands of years ago and returned to the sea. The earliest whale fossils are 40 million years old. Although they live entirely in water, they are still mammals because they give birth to live babies, nurse those babies, and breathe air with lungs, not gills. Their front limbs became paddles with no fingers and their back legs disappeared. The tail became a fin for swimming. They are also considered large vertebrates because they have spines.

Like owls and wasps, whales are carnivores. Some types of whales have teeth but others (baleen whales) have baleen plates made from sheets of something called keratin, the same material our fingernails are made of. Baleen, also called whalebone, hangs from the whale's upper jaw. The baleen of grey whales is grey with yellowish bristles that act like a filter. Because the ends of a whale's baleen are always wearing out, baleen grows throughout a whale's lifetime. The grey whale feeds mostly along the floor of the ocean, diving down and sucking in water, mud, and food, mostly marine worms and crustaceans. The whale closes its mouth and its tongue forces the water and mud out through the bristles of the baleen plates. Grey whales eat more than 1000 kilograms of food each day, and scientists have estimated that it takes 300 kilograms of food to fill a grey whale's stomach.

For more information:

http://www.enchantedlearning.com/subjects/whales/
   anatomy/Baleen.shtml

http://www.seaworld.org/infobooks/Baleen/
   dietbw.html

http://ecokids.earthday.ca/pub/eco_info/topics/
   whales/baleen_whales.cfm

ICE CUBE EXPERIMENT

Insulation can keep heat in—or out. For example, a thermos keeps cold drinks cold and hot drinks hot. This experiment lets you test how insulating your mitts are.

Materials:
* ✳ 3 ice cubes the same size
* ✳ 3 plastic sandwich bags (zip-lock ones are best)
* ✳ a thin woollen-type mitt or glove
* ✳ a thick ski-type mitt or glove

Procedure:
1. Place an ice cube in each of the bags and seal them.
2. Leave one ice cube in its bag sitting on the counter or table.
3. Place one inside the thin mitt or glove.
4. Place the last ice cube inside the thick ski mitt.
5. Every two to three minutes, check how much the ice has melted in each of the bags.

What Happened?

The ice cube that was sitting on the counter should have melted the fastest, while the ice cube in the ski mitt should have melted the slowest. Because there is a temperature difference between the room temperature and the ice cube, heat energy is transferred from the hotter place (the room) to the cooler place (the ice cube), thereby melting the ice cube until the temperature achieves thermal equilibrium. The two mitts you used acted as insulators to slow down the transfer of the room's heat energy to the ice cubes. The ski mitt, because of its thickness, was best able to slow the transfer of heat to the ice cube and therefore the ice cube in the ski mitt melted the slowest. The thin mitt was able to slow down the heat transfer somewhat, while the ice cube left on the counter had nothing to slow down the heat transfer. So it melted the fastest.

Just as the mitts can slow the transfer of heat from the room to the ice cubes, so the ice cubes can maintain their temperature longer; the mitts can also insulate your hands from cold temperatures outside. The mitts slow down the transfer of heat from your hands to the outside air, so they stay warmer. Obviously, the thicker ski mitt will do a better job than the thinner mitt.

Optional Experiment:

You can also make you own ice cube survival suit using materials you have at home that might act as good insulators. Any materials like bubble wrap, cloth, paper, Styrofoam, and so on, can be used. Make a few ice cube survival suits from different materials and see which one is the best insulator.

9

The Activist's Act

By the time they had biked home from the whale-watching excursion, the sun was touching the tops of the trees. Dropping her bike in the driveway, Sue rushed inside.

Nicole looked at Gina, confused. "What's she doing?"

"Maybe she had to go to the bathroom." Gina shrugged and wheeled her bike to the side of the cabin, then picked up Sue's and did the same.

When they got inside, Sue was not in the bathroom. She seemed to be tearing the cabin apart. The cushions were off the couch, the piles of magazines were skewed across the floor, and the small woodpile beside the stove was in pieces.

"Have you gone crazy?" Gina asked, restacking the magazines.

Sue's expression only grew more frantic. "I can't find the crystal. I had this idea while we were on the boat. I wanted to hang the crystal in the window. I thought the picture on the last page of the will might be a clue."

Understanding dawned first in Nicole's eyes. "The crystal might act like a prism, separating the light into a rainbow."

LIGHT AND PRISMS

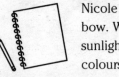

Nicole knew that prisms separate light into a rainbow. Why does that happen? It happens because sunlight is made up of a mixture of different colours, called the colour spectrum. The colours of the spectrum are the rainbow colours and always appear in the same order: red, orange, yellow, green, cyan (turquoise), blue, indigo, and violet, although the spectrum is actually a whole continuum of colours from red to violet. In *Science Squad #1*, we learned that light rays act like waves and have certain wavelengths. Each colour has a different wavelength. The longest wavelength is red. Orange is the next longest and so on. The shortest wavelength is violet. The human eye can detect wavelengths of the light spectrum between 400 nanometres (violet) and about 700 nanometres (red). One nanometre is about one millionth of a millimetre.

When all the different wavelengths of the colour spectrum reach your eye at the same time, you see white light. But when light passes through a prism (a triangular piece of glass), each wavelength is refracted (bent), causing dispersion of the white light into rainbow colours. Refraction is caused because the speed of light slows down as it hits more dense material

"Exactly. But I can't find the crystal!" Sue wailed.

Together, the three girls scoured the room again, with no results. Before they could put things back in order, Rose arrived home from her workshop.

(the prism), just like your speed slows down when you dive into the water. The light refracts again as it moves out of the prism. It speeds up as it moves from dense material (the prism) to less dense material (the air). Red, with the longest wavelength, bends the least, orange bends a little more and so on with each colour, all the way to violet, which bends the most. Because all the colours refract at different angles, the white light is dispersed into rainbow colours.

For more information:

http://www.colourware.co.uk/cpfaq/q1-1.htm

http://whyfiles.larc.nasa.gov/text/kids/Problem_Board/ problems/light/sim2.html

http://site.tekotago.ac.nz/staff/lgodman/drawing/info/ Tech/Lighting/Lightinga.html

"Do you have the crystal?" Sue immediately asked.

"The crystal? No. Why?" Rose looked at the girls curiously. "It looks like a tornado struck in here."

"We've been looking for it everywhere. If you don't have it, where could it have gone?" Gina replaced the couch cushions just in time for Sue to collapse on them dramatically.

"I had it out on the table this morning," Rose told them. "I thought I might hang it on the porch. But Tyler came over for coffee a little while ago, and I forgot about it."

Nicole moved to check the floor under the table one more time. There was no sign of the crystal.

Rose shrugged. "I'm sure it will show up. There's no sense worrying about it. There's a folk singer playing at the café in town tonight, and I was thinking of going. Anyone interested?"

Sue raised a hand from her swooning pose on the couch. "I'll go."

Nicole was about to agree, but Gina jumped in first. "Why don't you two have some family time together? I'd like the time to finish my wasp's nest model, and Nicole's really into her book."

• • •

As soon as Sue and Rose were out the door, Gina sprang into motion. "It's time to put our Internet skills to work again," she told Nicole as she started up the computer. "We've got to find out everything we can about Tyler."

"Why?"

"Because it's *obvious* that he stole the crystal."

"Why would Tyler want the crystal? It doesn't do anything. It's not even valuable."

"We know that," Gina said, "but maybe Tyler doesn't."

Obediently, Nicole sat in front of the computer and began a search for his name. It yielded some hockey scores from the Tofino arena, but not much else. Next, she found the home page of the local newspaper, where she could search the news archives. There was no mention of Tyler.

"That seems strange," Gina muttered from behind her shoulder. "Wouldn't an activist get his name in the news sometimes?"

Patiently, Nicole looked for the home pages of local environmental agencies. Within each page, she looked again for Tyler's name.

"I've got something!" she called, finally. Gina had wandered into the kitchen to put frozen pizzas in the oven. "This is last year's annual report from the Rain Forest Survival Network. Tyler's listed as a contract worker."

"Does it give a phone number for the network?" Gina asked.

As soon as Nicole read out the number, Gina dialled. Luckily, someone was working late.

"Rain Forest Survival Network," a man's voice answered.

"Hello. I'm checking references for a volunteer group in Nanaimo," Gina said, trying to sound older than she was. "I'm looking for information about Tyler Riley. I understand he used to work for your organization."

The man on the other end of the line seemed to pause.

"If you have any information that would be helpful, I assure you we will keep it confidential," Gina said, crossing her fingers.

"Well, I suppose technically he worked for us," the man answered, finally. "He had a contract to clean the offices after hours. But I can't say I'd give him a reference."

"Why is that?" Gina asked, using her most professional voice.

"We fired him a couple months ago. Couldn't prove anything, but we're pretty sure he was pocketing donations."

"Stealing?" Gina tried to keep her voice level.

"Let's just say he was soliciting donations for his own pocket, rather than the rain forest."

RAINBOWS

Rainbows are beautiful natural phenomena, but how do they occur? A number of things have to happen before a rainbow can form. First, it has to be raining in one part of the sky, and the sun has to be shining in another. To *see* a rainbow, the sun must be behind you. Finally, the angle at which the sunlight hits the back of the raindrop has to be just right. The rainbow is caused by refraction and reflection in falling water droplets. If the sunlight hits the back of the raindrop at an angle greater than 48 degrees, the light will be reflected back. If the angle is less than 48 degrees, the light will pass through the raindrop. As the light moves out of the raindrop, it is passing from denser material (the water) into less dense material. Reviewing the information from pp. 102–103, this means that the reflected light will refract (bend) as it leaves the raindrop. Also remember that violet light refracts the most. It exits the raindrop at a 40-degree angle (see diagram). Red light refracts the least and exits the raindrop at a 42-degree angle. All the other colours exit the raindrop at angles somewhere in between. Since you see only one colour of light from each raindrop, an incredible number of raindrops are required to produce the beautiful spectrum of colours that make up the rainbow.

For more information:

http://hyperphysics.phy-astr.gsu.edu/hbase/atmos/ rbowfeat.html

http://www.usatoday.com/weather/tg/wrainbow/ wrainbow.htm

http://dmoz.org/Kids_and_Teens/School_Time/Science/ The_Earth/Weather/Rainbows/

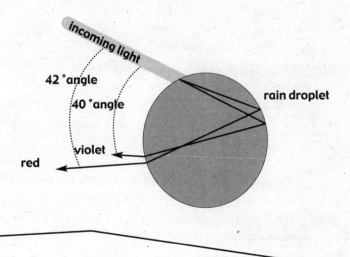

Quickly thanking the man, Gina hung up the phone and updated Nicole. "I knew it!" she concluded. "I knew he was up to something."

The oven timer buzzed and Gina pulled out their pizzas. The food couldn't distract them, however. They couldn't stop thinking about Tyler and the crystal.

"We have to find a way to get the crystal back and expose him as a fraud," Nicole said.

A couple hours later, the girls had gathered a pad of paper, some pens, and a couple of flashlights and retreated to the tree platform to plan. It was completely dark by the time they arrived and the owls were awake and active. This time, Nicole and Gina refused to be distracted.

"We should definitely call the police," Gina said.

"It won't work." Nicole shook her head firmly, her curls swinging. "First, the crystal is worthless. The police won't waste their time on it. Second, we have no proof that Tyler's a fake."

They sat for a few minutes in silence. "We could send him out to dinner with Rose," Nicole suggested. "Then sneak into his house and look for the crystal."

"Then the police will be interested," Gina said, rolling her eyes. "Because we'll be breaking and entering! No. We are not going into Tyler's house. Besides, that wouldn't prove he was a fraud. It would only prove he took the crystal."

Silence again, until there was a loud crashing in the bushes below. They heard footsteps on the ladder, and finally the whoosh of the zip line. Sue soon crashed to a stop on the platform, her gold hair glowing in the flashlight beams.

"The show's over," she said with a smile. "I figured you two were probably scheming without me."

Gina quickly filled her in on their discoveries. "So now we

have to find proof. And we have no idea how to do that."

Sue raised her eyebrows and offered them a wicked grin. "No problem," she said. ★

COMPUTERS

 Nicole probably doesn't realize that although personal computers are recent inventions, the fundamentals of programming developed over the past 200 years. Augusta Ada Byron King, Countess of Lovelace, was born in 1815 and was the only child of the English poet Lord Byron. Her parents separated when she was one month old, and she never saw her father again. Ada's mother, Lady Byron, didn't want her daughter to be a poet like her father, so she made sure Ada was tutored in mathematics and music. At a dinner party, Ada was introduced to a mathematician and inventor named Charles Babbage. Charles was working on a computer-like mechanical machine he called the Analytical Engine.

Charles presented his plans for his Analytical Engine at a seminar in Italy. His description was summarized and published in French by Italian mathematician Louis Menebrea. Ada translated the French article into English and, at Charles' suggestion, added her own notes, which made the article three times longer than the original article. Charles had written the part about how the machine could do certain mathematical calculations. However, Ada asked him to alter the plans because she had detected a big error. This plan is now considered to be an early "computer program."

Ada's article was published in 1843. In it she predicted many different uses for the machine. Even though Charles never built the machine, Ada predicted that in the future an analytical machine could also produce graphics and be used for practical and scientific purposes. Although people have been debating the extent of Ada's contribution to the early computer program, in 1979 a software language developed by the American Defence Department was named "Ada" in her honour.

For more information:

http://www.sdsc.edu/ScienceWomen/lovelace.html
http://www.well.com/user/adatoole/bio.htm
http://www.agnesscott.edu/lriddle/women/love.htm

"WHITE LIGHT" EXPERIMENT

This easy-to-make fan will help you understand white light and the colour spectrum.

Materials:
* sheet of white paper
* ruler
* scissors
* coloured crayons, pencils, or felt pens in the rainbow colours of red, orange, yellow, green, cyan (turquoise), blue, indigo, and violet

Procedure:

1. Cut the paper into a 16 x 18-cm rectangle.
2. With the ruler, measure off and mark 8 dots 2 cm apart along the length of the paper.
3. Use these dots to draw 8 vertical lines on the paper so that you end up with 9 columns 2 cm wide along the length of the paper.
4. Fold the paper back and forth along the 8 vertical lines the way you would to make a fan (see diagram).
5. Close the fan and note the top and bottom columns. You will keep these white.
6. Open the fan and now colour each column starting with the second column on the left. Colour the first column red, the next column orange, the next yellow, then green, cyan, blue, indigo, and violet as shown in diagram.
7. Hold the bottom of the fan closed between your thumb and index finger, as shown in the diagram.
8. Using your right thumb, bend the fan over at the base of the fan so it forms a right angle.

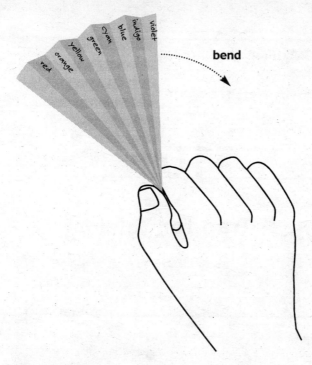

bend

What Happened?

When all the different wavelengths of the colour spectrum reach your eye at the same time, you see white light just as you would see when your fan is closed and only the white ends of the fan are visible. When light passes through a prism, each wavelength is refracted (bent), causing dispersion of the white light into rainbow colours the way you would see when you opened your fan. When you bent your fan over to the right, the red column would be bent the least and the violet column would be bent the most. This is how white light bends when it passes through a prism. Red, with the longest wavelength, bends the least, orange bends a little more, and so on, all the way to violet, which bends the most. Your fan gives you an example of how all the colours refract at different angles and white light is dispersed into rainbow colours.

10

A Trap for Tyler

Gina and Sue leaned against the wall of the alley, trying their best to look casual.

"He might see us here," Gina worried.

"He's not going to be searching in alleyways," Sue reassured her. "His mind will be on other things...like crystal."

"What if he took it to the jeweller last night?"

"Rose said he came for coffee just before dinner. The stores would have been closed until this morning."

"Is Nicole ready?"

Sue carefully leaned around the corner and peered down the street. Sitting on a bench in front of the jewellery store was a petite woman in a raincoat and hat. She looked nothing like Nicole. "She's there," Sue told Gina. "And her disguise is perfect."

As they watched, Nicole opened her purse and rummaged for a

small, mirrored compact. She appeared to check her lipstick before snapping the compact shut and glancing around, as if she were waiting for a bus. A few minutes later, she repeated the process.

The jeweller had been open for half an hour and Nicole had "checked her lipstick" a dozen times when she finally saw Tyler in her mirror. Nicole waited until he had gone inside before she took off her hat and shook out her curls. Not hurrying, she slung her purse over her shoulder and tucked her hat in her jacket pocket before following Tyler into the jewellery store.

"I thought I could get it appraised…." Tyler was saying, when the jingle of the door interrupted him. Both he and the jeweller turned to find Nicole smiling at them. She detected a flash of anger in Tyler's eyes, then his face was smooth.

"Oh, you've got our crystal," Nicole said, smiling at him sweetly. "We were wondering where that went."

"I knew you girls were…busy," he said, with a hint of sarcasm. "I thought it might help to have the crystal appraised."

"That's so sweet of you," Nicole cooed. "But the jeweller was nice enough to see us yesterday."

The jeweller nodded agreeably. "I was sorry to tell the young ladies that the crystal is worth very little. A mere decoration, I'm afraid."

Tyler's face fell into a scowl, and this time he didn't try to hide it.

"Thanks again," Nicole chirped. "Why don't I take this back to Rose for you?" She scooped up the crystal and dropped it into her purse before Tyler could object. Still playing dumb, she invited him to the cabin for dinner and swept out of the store. She had to force herself to walk, not run, into the alley to meet Sue and Gina.

Once the girls stopped giggling, Sue herded them home to test her theory.

MIRRORS AND REFLECTED LIGHT

Nicole was using her mirrored compact to spy on what was going on behind her. If you remember from *Science Squad #1* (pp. 42–43), light acts like waves and is often called rays. A reflection is a change in direction of a ray when it bounces off a surface. Mirrors have flat, smooth surfaces. So when parallel rays bounce off the smooth surface of Nicole's mirror, the rays stay parallel. This is called regular reflection. Because the rays stay parallel, a clear image is formed of the object the mirror is reflecting. The image (reflection) that is formed in a mirror is the same size as the object it is reflecting and it looks the same distance "inside" the mirror as the object really is to the mirror.

One other thing happens to the image. If you look in a mirror when you are wearing a T-shirt with writing on it, what do you notice? The writing is backwards because the image is reversed. This reversed image is said to be laterally inverted.

When parallel rays bounce off a rough surface, the rays travel in different directions and are scattered. Because the rays are scattered in all directions, no image (reflection) is formed. This is called diffuse reflection and is the most common type of reflection.

For more information:

http://camillasenior.homestead.com/optics3.html
http://www.opticalres.com/kidoptx.html#LightBasics
http://physics.bu.edu/~duffy/PY106/Reflection.html

"While you two were snoring in the Zodiac yesterday, I was watching the rainbows created by the spray from the bow," she explained, once back in the kitchen.

"I do not snore," Gina said primly.

"When light passes through prisms, like those little drops of water, it creates rainbows, right?" Sue continued.

Gina and Nicole nodded.

"This crystal should also act as a prism. If we hang it in the window…" Sue climbed on the kitchen counter as she talked. Using the fishing line attached to the crystal, she looped it over the curtain rod.

"Voila!" she said, stepping back.

In the midday sun, the prism sent a spray of colours across the kitchen. On the white-washed wood panelling that formed the cabin's interior walls, the colours looked especially bright. Nicole waved her hands in front of the crystal, watching rainbows dance on her skin. "This is the window that Rose's uncle drew on the third page of the will," she said.

Sue beamed. "I knew it must be important somehow. I think this is it." She started a twirling dance through the room.

"What do you mean this is it?" Gina protested. "It looks nice, but I wouldn't call this useful, or valuable. We've just decorated the kitchen."

Sue stopped twirling. "It has to point to something. I'm sure of it. Let's stand back and look where the light falls when the crystal is still."

For a moment, they stood together in one corner of the kitchen. "There," Sue pointed. "Look how that one string of light lines up exactly across that one board of the wall. I bet the uncle's treasure is hidden behind the panelling."

Gina shook her head doubtfully, but Sue ignored her. She

117

tapped the wall lightly. "It sounds hollow!" With her fingernails, she tried to grip one corner of the board and pry it loose, but it was nailed on too tightly.

"You need some sort of crowbar," Nicole said, grabbing a butter knife from the drawer. "Try this."

Working the edge of the knife into the gap between the boards, Sue was able to pry the board up slightly. She moved the knife over a few centimetres and tried again.

"You're ruining the kitchen," Gina told her, backing out of the room with her arms crossed. "If you're wrong—"

"I'm not wrong," Sue insisted, diligently working the knife along the corner of the board. Eventually, it was lifted enough that she could slip her fingers below and pull the board away from the wall. The middle of the board split with a loud crack.

"I want it officially on the record that I was against this," Gina said.

Finally the board tore away with a cracking sound, to reveal… nothing. There was only a small gap between the vertical wood studs that framed the wall.

"Something has to be here," Sue insisted, feeling all sides of the gap.

"You'd better find it quickly or prepare to explain this to Rose," Gina called from the living room. "Because she just pulled into the driveway. And Tyler's with her!" ★

HOLLOW-SOUNDING WALLS

Why did Sue say that the wall sounded hollow when she tapped the wall? She probably heard a louder, lower thud sound, which should indicate a hollow behind the wall. A quieter, higher, or more solid sound would indicate a stud or obstruction inside the wall. Remember that sound travels in waves. Also remember that the amplitude of a sound wave is the distance between the top of the crest and the rest position (centre line), or the bottom of the trough and the rest position (centre line). Amplitude determines volume or how loud a sound is. The frequency of a wave is the number of wavelengths per a certain unit of time. Frequency determines pitch, or how high or low the sound is.

Sound waves create air vibrations and these air vibrations in turn will vibrate walls. When Sue knocked where the wall was hollow, that part of the wall acted like a big drum and vibrated at a lower frequency but a higher amplitude. The lower the frequency, the lower the pitch and the lower the sound. The higher the amplitude, the louder the sound. If Sue knocked where there was a wooden stud or a solid obstruction, the area would be more rigid and wouldn't produce as much vibration. The amplitude would be lower but the frequency would be higher. This would make the sound quieter but higher. By listening to the different sounds as Sue tapped on the wall, she was able to determine which part sounded hollow.

For more information:

**http://whyfiles.larc.nasa.gov/text/kids/Problem_Board/
   problems/sound/sound_waves2.html**

**http://www.yale.edu/ynhti/curriculum/units/2000/5/
   00.05.05.x.html#c**

SIMPLE MACHINES

 In Chapter 2, Rose used a simple machine, the pulley, to make the zip line. Nicole found another simple machine—the butter knife. Nicole knew that Sue needed something like a crowbar to use as a lever. The butter knife would do the trick! Simple machines help make better use of muscle power to do work because a machine can overcome a force, called the load. Levers are one of the simplest types of simple machines and have been used for thousands of years. In fact, we probably don't even realize how often we use levers in our everyday lives.

The lever is usually made from some rigid bar and has three components: 1) the effort, 2) the load or resistance, and 3) the fulcrum. The effort is the push or pull (force) applied to the lever. (A force is needed to make a machine like a lever work.) The load or resistance refers to the weight of the object the lever moves. The fulcrum is the fixed point where the lever pivots. (Think of the support on which the long board of a teeter-totter is balanced as a type of fulcrum.) All levers use effort, load, and a fulcrum. There are three types of levers and they are called first-class, second-class, and third-class. The levers are differentiated by how the effort, load, and fulcrum are ordered in relation to one another.

In a first-class lever, the fulcrum is positioned somewhere between the effort and the load, like in a teeter-totter where the effort and load move in opposite directions. For example, when you push down on one side of a teeter-totter (the effort), the other side (the load) goes up. How close the fulcrum is to the effort or load will affect the force you need and the speed and distance the load side travels. Thinking back to your teeter-totter, when you move the board so the fulcrum is closer to you, you will need to apply more force to make the load move, but the load will move a greater distance and speed. This means the person (the load) sitting opposite you on the teeter-totter will move faster and go higher. When you move the board so the fulcrum is farther from you, you will need to apply less force, but the load will move a smaller distance and at a lower speed.

In a second-class lever, the load is between the effort and fulcrum. Bottle openers, nutcrackers, and wheelbarrows are examples of second-class levers. Unlike the first-class lever, the second-class lever doesn't change the direction of the effort; both the effort and the load move in the same direction. When the fulcrum is closer to the load than to the effort, as it is with a bottle opener, it takes less effort to move the load (the bottle cap).

In a third-class lever, the effort is between the load and the fulcrum. Hockey sticks, tennis rackets, brooms, and shovels are examples of third-class levers. With third-class levers, the effort is applied between the fulcrum and the load. When you use these "levers," you apply the effort, your hands are the fulcrum, and the load is the puck you are hitting or the dirt you are sweeping. Third-class levers need more effort to move the load because the load must move through a greater distance than the effort, but the load will move with greater speed, which is what you want when you are hitting a puck or tennis ball.

Sue was using the butter knife as a first-class lever. The fulcrum was the edge of the board on which Sue rested the middle part of the knife. The load was the board she was trying to lift and Sue's hands were applying the effort. So the fulcrum was positioned between the effort and the load, like in a teeter-totter, and the effort and load moved in opposite directions. Sue was pushing on the end of the butter knife to pull up the board.

For more information:

http://207.10.97.102/elscizone/lessons/land/
    simplmachines/3classes.htm

http://www.fi.edu/pieces/knox/automaton/lever.htm

http://www.san-marino.k12.ca.us/~summer1/machines/
    simplemachines.html

SOUND WAVES AND HOLLOW WALL EXPERIMENT

Try what Sue did and see if you can determine where your walls are hollow and where they are not.

Materials:

⚹   inside walls of your house

Procedure:

1. Use your knuckles and gently knock on your walls.
2. Notice the difference in sounds, particularly as you knock close to the corners of walls and beside windows and door frames.

What Happened?

When you knocked close to corners of walls and beside windows and door frames, you would have heard a higher pitched but quieter sound than when you knocked in the middle of the walls. A lower and louder thud sound should indicate a hollow behind the wall. A quieter, higher, or more solid sound would indicate a stud or obstruction inside the wall. This is because sound waves create air vibrations, and these air vibrations in turn will vibrate walls. When you knock where the wall is hollow, that part of the wall acts like a big drum and vibrates at a lower frequency but a higher amplitude, making the sound lower and louder. When you knock where there is a wooden stud or a solid obstruction, the area will be more rigid and won't produce as much vibration. The amplitude will be lower but the frequency will be higher, making the sound quieter but higher.

11

Con-fessions

Sue was the last to land on the tree platform, still breathless from the jog up the trail.

"Do you think they saw us leaving?" Gina asked.

Sue grimaced. "I jammed the board back into the wall and followed you out the back door before they were even inside. They were still playing tonsil hockey on the front porch."

"That's just disgusting," Nicole protested. "Rose should know she's kissing a snake."

"We should know it's none of our business," Gina replied, adopting her most mature look.

"She's my aunt. That makes it my business," Sue said vehemently. "And I'm going to prove that Tyler's a fake—as soon as you two stop chatting and help me start scheming." Their heads close together, the Science Squad began brainstorming.

• • •

"That book you found in the library was so helpful," Gina said to Nicole over the pasta dinner that Rose had prepared.

"Who would have thought that one piece of information about prisms could be so important?" Gina continued. Watching Tyler from the corner of her eye, she could tell she had captured his attention.

"And what information is that?" Rose asked, her lips pursed in disapproval. She offered Tyler an exasperated smile. "I swear these girls are determined to solve the world's mysteries. Personally, I'm beginning to think this is just one of my uncle's usual tricks. He's left me a lovely carved box, a crystal, and a sketch."

Tyler agreed. "Maybe those were the gifts he meant you to have."

Gina watched as Nicole forced a fake smile and redirected the conversation back to the library book. "I forgot the book on the tree platform, and it's difficult to explain what we found. I can show it to you tomorrow," she told Rose.

Groaning, Sue pushed her empty plate away. "That was great, but I'm stuffed. Can we walk to the road and back before we do the dishes? I need a few minutes of exercise."

Rose excused them, and the girls rushed out the door. The sun was beginning to set, and shadows stretched across the driveway. Once out of sight of the house, they raced to the bushes below the tree platform. Sue had already scouted a perfect hiding place.

It was only a few minutes before they heard footsteps on the path. Nicole gripped Gina's arm in excitement.

"Stay still," Gina breathed. "A couple more seconds."

It was hard to see the path from where they were hidden, but listening carefully they heard footsteps pass them and start up the ladder. Gina waited two more minutes.

125

FEELING FULL AFTER EATING

 Eating is very important for the health and survival of animals (us included). But how do we know how much to eat, and when to stop eating? That's easy! We eat until our stomachs are full. Or do we? Actually, it depends on the food. Adults are programmed to eat "the right amount" to meet their current needs and keep their body weight relatively constant. But "the right amount" doesn't mean the right volume or quantity of food; it means the right amount of nutrition we get from our food. So if an animal (or you!) eats something very nutritious, it may stop eating when its stomach is only half full. But if it eats an equal volume or quantity of food that isn't nutritious, it will keep eating. This has led scientists to believe that the walls of our stomach contain receptors (specialized nerve cells) sensitive to the nutrients in our foods. If we eat something nutritious, the receptors in our stomachs may send signals to the brain telling it that nutrients are on the way. The result: we feel full.

Most people will feel full about 10 minutes after they begin eating, but for those who are obese, it may take almost twice as long for their brains to get the message that they are full. Brain research is finding that the programming in the brain to tell us to *stop* eating is less developed than that which tells us to start. Additional research has found that overeating and obesity produce changes in the brain. This occurs because overeating can affect changes in the pleasure-reinforcement parts of the brain. It's important to realize that lots of sweet and fatty junk food didn't exist thousands of years ago when people ate mostly meat, roots, and nuts with occasional fruit and vegetables, not potato chips and chocolate bars. However, these delicious (if far from nutritious) foods have changed the way our brains process food information. Most of us don't eat only when we're hungry or starving. Most of us eat because we enjoy it. The brain has a lot of programming to reinforce eating. But those programs to tell us to stop have not kept up with the abundant supply of tasty junk food.

For more information:

http://www.eufic.org/gb/food/pag/food33/food332.htm
http://www.3d-edu.com/h&f.htm

"Now!" she whispered to Nicole, who leapt up as quietly as speed would allow and scampered up the ladder. Halfway up, she heard the thunk of someone landing on the opposite platform. Reaching as high as she could, Nicole jammed a stick into the pulley at her end. The zip line was now out of commission.

"Done," she called down, secrecy no longer so important.

"Is the camera flashing?" Sue asked.

Nicole looked over to the opposite platform. After a minute, she saw a short burst of light. Sue had managed to attach a small motion detector to her camera and hang both from an overhead branch, just out of reach from the platform. As Tyler moved, the camera snapped images.

"It's working," Nicole yelled back to Sue. Gina didn't really see the point in the pictures. If all went well, the tape recorder in Nicole's pocket would be more than enough to incriminate Tyler. Still, Sue had managed to snap shots of every mystery they had solved so far.

"Hey! What's going on?" Tyler began to yell. He tested the zip line and found it jammed.

Smiling smugly to herself, Gina picked her way through the brush until she was below the platform. "Stay calm up there, Tyler. We have some questions for you."

Not waiting to hear what questions Gina asked, Sue sprinted back along the path to the cabin. "Rose! Can you come to the tree platform? We've trapped Tyler," she gasped.

"You've what?" Her face immediately creased with worry, Rose hurried outside.

Sue followed at her heels feeling like an overexcited puppy. "We had to prove he's a fake. We said those things about the new prism discovery to see if he would go to the tree platform and try to steal the book. And he did!"

SHADOWS AND PYRAMIDS

 The girls rushed outdoors just as the sun was beginning to set and probably didn't even pay attention to the shadows stretching across the driveway. They would have been very interested to learn that shadows can be used to measure the height of very tall structures without having to climb to the top of the structure. This method of using shadows is called shadow reckoning and was discovered as an important measurement tool more than 2500 years ago. Shadow reckoning was used extensively by the ancient Greeks to measure the height of objects that could not easily be measured.

Thales was a great mathematician who lived in Greece about 2600 years ago. When Thales visited Egypt, he was able to amaze the citizens by using shadow reckoning to measure the height of one of the pyramids. Egyptian pyramids are enormous, beautiful, triangular structures built more than 4500 years ago. During that time, people thought there was no easy way to measure the height of pyramids. But Thales used a simple method to measure it by measuring his shadow at different times of the day. At the time of day when his shadow became equal to his own height, he quickly measured the length of the shadow cast by the pyramid. Since at that point in time his own height was the same size as his shadow, the pyramid shadow would be the same size as its height. In that way, he was able to estimate the height of the pyramid.

For more information:

http://educ.queensu.ca/~fmc/april2002/Pyramids.htm
http://uzweb.uz.ac.zw/science/maths/zimaths/
42/estima.htm

Rose grimaced, slowing to look back at Sue. "Are you sure? He said he had an important meeting to get to."

"I'm completely sure."

When they arrived back at the platform, Gina had her hands on her hips and she was smirking with self-satisfaction.

"He's not an environmentalist at all," she told Rose. "He's admitted that he was part of the crew on a fishing boat and he jumped ship when they docked in Tofino. They may be interested in finding the money he stole when he left."

"It was only petty cash," Tyler yelled down. "I was seasick. And I had to eat, didn't I?"

"What about the theft from the environmental group?" Sue called up.

"I need to pay my way back to California, dude," he said. "The weather up here's killin' me. But those donations to the rain forest were pitiful—it was taking me forever to get any cash. If you girls hadn't interfered, the money from the will would have been perfect."

"Don't you mean 'primo, dude?'" Sue asked, making Gina roll her eyes.

"I guess his surfer dude image has worn thin."

Rose took a step forward to stand beside the girls. When she spoke, her voice was cold and firm. "I think we've established that there is no will money," she said. "We have also established that you are not the person I thought. Since the girls have trapped you up there so efficiently, I think you may as well stay there until the police arrive."

Barely suppressing their smiles, the girls watched as Rose flipped open her cellphone to call the police. When she hung up, Sue found the rope pulley she'd attached to her camera and lowered it from the nearby tree. Nicole handed over the tape recorder from inside her jacket.

Rose accepted both, shaking her head in astonishment. "You girls think of everything, don't you? Nice work."

"We tried to tell you that he was a fake," Sue said.

Rose offered her a rueful grin. "Looks like I should have listened."

"Let's all just chill for a while and work this out. We could have split the money once I found it! I just needed a plane ticket!" Tyler was still protesting from above when the girls heard the sound of a police siren in the distance. ★

SEASICKNESS

Seasickness is a type of motion sickness. The symptoms are nausea and often vomiting and unsteadiness. Motion sickness can occur when a person's position sensors receive conflicting messages. Humans and most animals have position sensors that continually provide our brains with information about movement. These sensors are our eyes, structures in our joints, tendons and muscles, and fluid-filled balance organs in our inner ears. When working together properly, these sensors keep us from falling down.

Our inner ears have a fluid-filled section lined with tiny hairs important for balance and the position of our heads. When our heads move, the fluid in the inner ears moves too. The movement of fluid causes the tiny hair cells to move. The tiny hair cells are actually receptors, so when they move they send messages to the brain. The brain interprets this information and uses it to figure out where our head is positioned. Our brain not only relies on the inner ear for its position and balance information, it has other sources of information too. One of these is our eyes. Our image of the world changes as we move our heads, so our brain uses information from our eyes as well when interpreting position information. Motion sickness can occur when this information conflicts. If you are reading a book in a car, your inner ear will be picking up information about the movement of the car, but your eyes will only be seeing the pages of the book. Or if you are sitting inside a moving boat, your inner ear will once again be picking up the movement information of the boat, but your eyes do not detect this movement because they see the inside of the boat, which is moving along with you. The information does not seem to agree. It is these types of situations that can cause motion sickness.

For more information:

http://kidshealth.org/kid/talk/qa/motion_sickness.html
http://kidshealth.org/kid/body/ear_noSW_p3.html
http://hyperphysics.phy-astr.gsu.edu/hbase/sound/
  eari.html#c3
http://www.ncf.carleton.ca/boating/seasickness.html
http://www.physsportsmed.com/issues/2000/05_00/
  scuba.htm

TALL OBJECTS EXPERIMENT

Try this experiment to estimate the height of some tall objects the way Thales did. This is an outdoor activity and needs two people. It also needs a large, level area, like a field or park, surrounding the object you want to measure.

Materials:

* ⚹ tape measure
* ⚹ small objects like sticks or stones to use as markers
* ⚹ paper and pencil
* ⚹ outdoor field or park
* ⚹ sunny day (for shadows)

Procedure:

1. Choose a tall object you want to measure, like a tree or telephone pole.
2. Stand in the sunshine and have someone place two small objects you are using as markers at both ends of your shadow, one by your feet and another marker by your head.
3. Using the tape measure, measure the length of your shadow and record the length on the piece of paper (A in diagram).
4. Measure your height in upright position and record your height on the piece of paper (B in diagram).

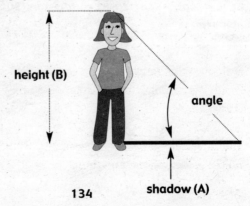

height (B)

angle

shadow (A)

5. At the same time of day, mark the end of the shadow of the object you want to measure with another marker.

6. Using the tape measure, measure the length of your object's shadow and record the length on the piece of paper (C in diagram).

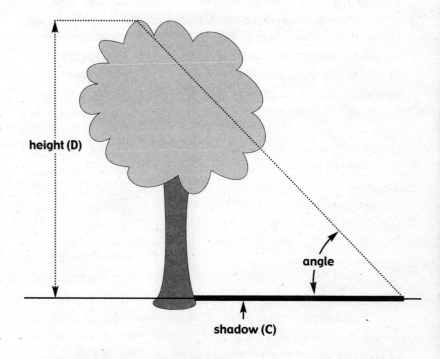

height (D)

angle

shadow (C)

7. Multiply your height by the length of the object's shadow. Divide this number by the length of your own shadow so that

$$D = \frac{C \times B}{A}$$

8. The final calculation is the estimate of the height of the tall object you wanted to measure.

What Happened?

When you measure your own shadow and the shadow of the object you want to measure at the same time of day, the sun is a fixed point in the sky. Because the sun is so far away, we can assume that the sun rays are parallel. Therefore, the sun is making the same angle with level ground and we have two similar triangles as shown in the diagram. Because the two triangles are the same shape, we know mathematically that the lengths and heights of both triangles are proportional to each other, meaning that the proportion (ratio) of your height (B) to your shadow length (A) is the same as the proportion (ratio) of the object's height (D) to the object's shadow length (C). To write these proportions mathematically, we would write:

$$\frac{D}{C} = \frac{B}{A}$$

where:

D is unknown

Solving for D

$$= \frac{C \times B}{A}$$

As an example, say you want to measure the height of a tree in a park. Your height is 120 cm; B = 120. Your shadow length is 80 cm; A = 80. The tree's shadow is 400 cm; C = 400. The estimated height of your tree would be 400 x 120 = 48000 ÷ 80 = 600 cm.

12

End of the Rainbow

"Gina! Nicole! Come here, quick!" The girls woke to Sue calling them from the kitchen. They stumbled out of their room in their pyjamas, and Rose wandered out as well, rubbing her eyes.

"This better be good," Gina grumbled.

Sue was so excited she could barely get her words out. Watching her bounce up and down was like watching a yo-yo. It began to make Gina dizzy.

"I woke up early," Sue rambled. "Making tea. I was pouring the water in the kettle and—look at the sun. Look at the sun!"

The girls looked out the window in confusion.

Obviously exasperated by their blank looks, Sue bounded into the living room and came back with a piece of paper. It was the final page of the will. "Look!" she said, pointing to the illustration, then to the kitchen window.

"We know," Nicole said. "They're the same."

Sue groaned dramatically. "But look at the sun beams. In the illustration, they're at exactly this angle. We were right when we hung the prism here. We just have to hang it at the proper time of day."

"And that's now!" Understanding filled Gina's eyes, and she raced for the prism. When she returned and hung it from the curtain rod, the specs of light floated only in one corner of the room.

Rose looked doubtful. "You want to tear up *another* wall of my kitchen?" The girls had only admitted to breaking the first board late the night before.

"We were right about Tyler, weren't we?" Sue adopted a winning smile.

When Rose finally gave a short nod, the girls set to work. Sue tapped the wall until she found a spot that sounded hollow, then Gina carefully pried up a corner of the board.

"There's something there!" she called.

"Let me see." Squeezing her way past the girls, Rose reached behind the wall to pull out a canvas-wrapped package. She slowly unfolded it.

"What is it?" Nicole whispered.

Rose looked up, her eyes wide with shock. "They're savings bonds in my uncle's name. There's more than enough here to pay the property taxes for the next two or three years. By that time, maybe I'll know what to do with the land."

Sue squealed with excitement and threw herself at Rose for a hug. When she calmed down slightly, Gina cleared her throat.

"I know what you might want to do with the property," she said to Rose. "I couldn't sleep this morning, so I took my sketches of the owls and did some research on the Internet. They're spotted owls."

"Aren't they endangered?" Rose asked.

"They're threatened by settlement and logging," Gina told her. "There are only twenty or thirty pairs still nesting in B.C. If you can set this land aside as a wildlife refuge, you may be able to run it as a non-profit organization."

"A non-profit refuge—that wouldn't count as commercial use of the land, but it would still bring in donations. They would help pay the property taxes," Rose nodded.

"Do you think it'll work?" Sue asked, bounding around the room in excitement.

"It's worth a try," Rose smiled. "You girls have given me and the owls a new purpose."

• • •

"I'm going to miss Rose," Sue said as the ferry approached Horseshoe Bay at the outskirts of Vancouver.

"I'm going to miss Tofino." Nicole sighed. "No more orienteering lessons. No more surfing. We're back to school in three days."

"I talked to my mom on the phone last night and she's coming to pick us up," Gina said. "Before we see her, you two have to promise not to tell her that we got lost in the rain forest. She'll never let me go on vacation again!"

The girls agreed, laughing as they remembered how overprotective Gina's mom could be. Linking arms, they started down the overhead walkway toward the parking lot. Soon they saw a familiar minivan and Gina's mom waving a warm welcome.

Sue gave one final sigh. "Back to the world of parents and homework. Do you think there's even the slightest chance of anything exciting happening?"

"I certainly hope not," Gina said immediately.

Nicole took a minute longer to decide. "This isn't very scientific," she said finally, "but my instincts tell me there are a few more mysteries to come." ★

139

NORTHERN SPOTTED OWLS

 Gina identified that the owls she had sketched were spotted owls. Her Internet research also found that because of declining habitat, northern spotted owls are endangered. It is hard to know how few owls are left. Estimates put the number in Canada at only 25–100 owls and some estimates suggest even fewer. Northern spotted owls like to live in forests that are more than 250 years old with many layers of tree canopy that are high and open enough to allow the owls to fly between and underneath the trees. Spotted owls also prefer areas of large trees with broken tops and large holes they can use for nesting.

Owls are carnivores. Northern spotted owls eat a variety of prey, including flying squirrels, birds, insects, reptiles, woodrats, mice, and other small rodents. Northern spotted owls are very territorial and do not like to have their habitat disturbed. Each pair of owls needs a large area of land for hunting and nesting. They use about 2.5–8 km^2 of old-growth forest areas. Pairs of males and females mate in February or March, and the female lays two or three white eggs in March or April. The female sits on the eggs for about 30 days. After the eggs hatch, the female sits with the babies for eight to 10 days. The mate helps out during this time. He catches and brings food to the female and babies. After hatching, it takes the young birds 34–36 days before they fledge—that is, get the feathers necessary for flying.

For more information:

http://www.enchantedlearning.com/subjects/birds/
   printouts/Spottedowlprintout.shtml

http://www.kidsplanet.org/factsheets/
   northspotowl.html

http://biology.usgs.gov/s+t/SNT/noframe/pn172.htm

http://earthobservatory.nasa.gov/Study/SpottedOwls/

WILDLIFE REFUGE

Gina knows how important it is to protect endangered species like the northern spotted owl. Loss of biodiversity, or species extinction, can affect all of us. There are two ways to prevent extinction of plant and animal species. The best way is to conserve species' habitats so they can continue to live in the wild. Many species, however, cannot survive by just being left alone. The second way to prevent extinction is to manage wild places. Often wild places can become degraded or disappear entirely. In many places, wildlife parks or nature conservation areas are being created to protect our species.

Gina suggested that Rose could set aside her land as a wildlife refuge. Refuges are a way to save and preserve many species. In 1986, the Committee on the Status of Endangered Wildlife in Canada made the northern spotted owl an endangered species. Unfortunately, this designation has limited usefulness because Canada has no endangered species legislation. In British Columbia, the owls are protected by the British Columbia Wildlife Act. This act forbids by law the possession, destruction, and injury to the bird, its nest, or its eggs, but it does not protect habitat. Unfortunately, the owls' habitats are being destroyed. The northern spotted owl doesn't normally breed in areas that have been cut and cleared of trees. Because large areas of forests have been cleared by logging, the numbers of northern spotted owls have declined. In various regions, attempts have been made to limit the legal sale of timber from the areas where the owls usually live. This has created conflict between some timber companies that want to log the timber and conservationists who want to protect old-growth forests and the species that live in them.

For more information:

http://www.nsnews.com/issues02/w100702/101302/
news/101302nn3.html

http://www.bcen.bc.ca/bcerart/Vol8/spottedo.htm

http://oregoncoast.fws.gov/capemeares/

HERBAL TEA EXPERIMENT

You can make tea from a variety of different herbs, fruits, and spices. You can make simple herbal teas from a single ingredient like mint, or more complex ones by mixing a number of different ingredients. Try experimenting a bit by making your own recipes following the directions below. Not all ingredients will taste good together. If you aren't sure what to mix together, here's a simple one to try: dried apple and dried sweetened cranberries, plus cinnamon and honey to taste. *Be sure you check with an adult before using ingredients for your experiment and make sure you are not allergic to any of the ingredients you use.*

Materials:

✷ variety of different herbs and dried fruit such as apples, cranberries, apricots, cinnamon, mint, ginger, rosemary, thyme, orange and lemon peel, and/or chamomile (You should be able to find some of these on the spice rack in your kitchen; others can be found at grocery stores.)

✷ teapot

✷ tea strainer

✷ measuring spoon

✷ tea cup or mug

✷ hot water

✷ lemon slice (optional)

✷ honey or sugar

Procedure:

1. Carefully choose the herbs or dried fruit you want to use. (Mixing too many together can make funny-tasting tea.)

2. If you use dried fruits, chop them into small pieces and mix

144

them together. If you are using herbs, make sure they are ground into small pieces.

3. Put 15 mL of dried herbs or fruit into the teapot for each cup of tea you plan to make. Then add 15 more mL to the teapot. If you want to make 2 cups of tea, you should have 45 mL of dried herbs or dried fruit in the teapot.

4. Boil water and carefully pour it into the teapot. Make sure you have enough water for the number of cups of tea you plan to make.

5. Replace the lid of the teapot and let contents steep for at least 5 minutes.

6. Pour through tea strainer into teacup. If the tea is not strong enough yet, let it sit for a few minutes longer.

7. Add fresh lemon if desired.

8. Add honey or sugar to taste.

9. Let the tea cool a bit so you don't burn your tongue, and taste your matsterpiece.

What Happened?

Normally when you put ingredients into water and let them dissolve, you are making a solution. The substance that dissolves is the solute, and the substance that dissolves the solute is the solvent (usually water). Since an entire apple chunk won't dissolve in water, we make an infusion. This means that the solids stay in the water, while the flavour, colour, and other molecules infuse into the water. Steeping is the soaking of a substance to extract its soluble properties. So steeping allows molecules from the tea ingredients to infuse into the water.

For more information:

http://www.tea.ca/

http://www.teahealth.co.uk/

Acknowledgements

The fictitious characters of "science Sue" and her original Science Squad were introduced in the first published newsletter of the Canadian Association for Girls In Science (CAGIS). Modelled after actual CAGIS members, these girls were interested in all aspects of science, technology, engineering and mathematics. In 1999, the founding president, Larissa Vingilis-Jaremko, and Dr. Evelyn Vingilis conceived of developing stories, based on the Science Squad, where the Squad used their science to solve mysteries. A grant from the Ministry of Energy, Science and Technology of Ontario provided the support to produce the Science Squad Webisodes, which formed the basis of the first book in this series.

The authors would like to thank Dr. John Wiebe for his help with some of the scientific content of this book. Michael Denton and BC Ferries helped provide facts about radar, and ferry navigation.

References

Ada Byron, Countess of Lovelace.
  URL: http://www.sdsc.edu/ScienceWome /lovelace.html.
  Accessed: March 30, 2003.

Adventures in Science Series. 1989. *How Things Work*. Educational
  Insights: Dominguez Hills, CA.

Adventures in Science Series. 1990. *Spy Science*. Educational Insights:
  Dominguez Hills, CA.

Amazing Egyptian Pyramids, The.
  URL: http://educ.queensu.ca/~fmc/april2002/Pyramids.htm.
  Accessed: April 5, 2003.

American Academy of Otolaryngology. Dizziness and Motion Sickness.
  URL: http://www.entnet.org/healthinfo/balance/dizziness.cf.
  Accessed: April 15, 2003.

American Council on Exercise. Fit Facts.
  URL: http://www.acefitness.org/fitfacts/fitfacts_display.cfm?itemid=55.
  Accessed: March 10, 2003.

Ask a Scientist Physics Archive.
  URL: http://newton.dep.anl.gove/askasci/phy99/psy99x34.htm.
  Accessed: January 1, 2003.

Augusta Ada King, Countess of Lovelace.
  URL: http://www-gap.dcs.st-and.ac.uk/~history/Mathematicians/
    Lovelace.html.
  Accessed: March 30, 2003.

Babbage Papers, The. Augusta Ada Lovelace.
  URL: http://www.ex.ac.uk/BABBAGE/ada.html.
  Accessed: March 30, 2003.

Barrett, S. 2001. *Lectures in Evolution.* Departments of Botany and
  Zoology, University of Toronto.

Beasant, P. 1992. *100 Facts about Space.* Kingfisher Books:
  New York, NY.

Beaudry, B. The Discovery of the Principle of the Thàles Theorem.
  URL: http://www.geocities.com/antidummy/sub/geeks/html.
  Accessed: April 5, 2003.

Bender, L. 1989. *The Human Factor: The World of Science.* Planned and
  produced by Equinox Ltd: Oxford. Published by Southside Publishing:
  Edinburgh, UK.

Brodeur, M. 2001. Mayday Relay. *Shorelines* 6(1).
  URL: http:///www.hypothermia.org/mayday/mayday.html.
  Accessed: March 12, 2003.

Bugline Winnipeg. Bees and Wasps.
  URL: http://www.winnipeg-bugline.com/bee.html.
  Accessed: March 9, 2003.

Buoyancy: Archimedes Principle.
URL: http://www.cei.net/~dvines/archem.htm.
Accessed: January 1, 2003.

Canadian Communities Atlas. Cultures and Ethnic Origins.
URL: http://cgdi.gc.ca/ccatlas/joamie/humgeog/culture/
culture.htm.
Accessed: April 5, 2003.

Canadian Inuit History: A Thousand Year Odyssey.
URL: http://www.civilization.ca/educat/oracle/modules/
dmorrison/page01_e.html.
Accessed: April 5, 2003.

Cassidy, J. 1991. *Explorabook: A Kids' Science Museum in a Book.* Klutz
Press: Palo Alto, CA.

Chen-See, S. 2003. "Bejeweled and Bedazzled." *YES MAG* 33,
Mar./Apr.: 8–9.

Coleman, B. and Van Vleet, D. The Northern Spotted Owl Debate.
URL: http://www.spa3.k12.sc.us/WebQuests/endangeredanimals/
endangered.htm.
Accessed: April 5, 2003.

Columbia Electronic Encyclopedia, The. 2002. Fact Monster.
© 2002 Family Education Network. Hives.
URL: http://www.factmonster.com/ce6/sci/A0823841.html.
Accessed: March 9, 2003.

Connecting Geometry. Similar Triangles.
URL: http://www.k12.hi.us/~csanders/ch_09Similar.html.
Accessed: April 5, 2003.

Davidson, Robert. 2002. Map Reading.
URL: http://www.map-reading.com/appendf.php.
Accessed: February 2, 2003.

Eaton, D. Trying to Keep the Diver Warm.
  URL: http://www.uhms-glc.ca/eaton.htm.
  Accessed: March 12, 2003.

Educational Insights. 1990. *Spy Science Adventures in Science Series*.
  Educational Insights: Dominguez Hills, CA.

Estimating Very Big Things.
  URL: http://uzweb.uz.ac.zw/science/maths/zimaths/42/
    estima.htm.
  Accessed: April 5, 2003.

First Nations. 1995. Coastal Temperate Rainforests.
  URL: http://www.inforain.org/rainforestatlas/index.htm.
  Accessed: January 16, 2003.

Golden Crown, The. Introduction.
  URL: http://www.mcs.drexel.edu/~crorres/Archimedes/
    Crown/CrownIntro.html.
  Accessed: March 3, 2003.

Gleitman, H. et al. 1999. *Psychology*. W.W. Norton & Company,
  New York.

Graff, J. 1997. Controlling Home Noise: Basics for Beginners.
  URL: http://www.uwex.edu/ces/pubs/pdf/B3239.PDF.
  Accessed: April 3, 2003.

Greensmiths. Bees and Wasps.
  URL: http://www.greensmiths.com/bees.htm.
  Accessed: March 9, 2003.

Harris, T. *How Fire Works*.
  URL: http://howstuffworks.com/fire1.htm.
  Accessed: February 24, 2003.

Helly Hanson Workwear Site. The Flotation Collection.
  URL: http://www.hhworkwear.com/products/flotation_survival/intro3.shtml.
  Accessed: March 12, 2003.

History of Cryptography.
    URL: http://www.cs.usask.ca/resources/tutorials/csconcepts/
        encryption/Lessons/L1/History.html.
    Accessed: February 23, 2003.

Information Center—FAQ. Fire Phenomena.
    URL: http://www.fs-business.com/InformationCenter/faq/
        FAQFirePhenomena.asp.
    Accessed: March 3, 2003.

Jones, B. 1991. *An Introduction to Practical Astronomy*. Chartwell Books:
    Secaucus, NJ.

KidsHealth. What's Motion Sickness?
    URL: http://kidshealth.org/kid/talk/qa/motion_sickness.html.
    Accessed: April 15, 2003.

Lady Augusta Ada Byron, Countess of Lovelace.
    URL: http://www.stsci/service/wsf/current/inventions.html.
    Accessed: November 11, 2000.

Lancaster, D. *North Shore News*.
    URL: http://www.nsnews.com/issues02/w100702/101302/news/
        101302nn3.html.
    Accessed: April 5, 2003.

Light and Optics. Submodule 3: Color and the Spectrum.
    URL: http://acept.la.asu.edu/PiN/mod/light/colorspectrum/
        pattLight3Obj3.html.
    Accessed: March 12, 2002.

London Fire. What Is Fire?
    URL: http://www.angliacampus.com/education/fire/
        secondar/fire.htm.
    Accessed: February 24, 2003.

Los Alamos National Laboratory. 1999. Periodic Table.
    URL: http://pearl1.lanl.gov/periodic/what.htm.
    Accessed: February 23, 2003.

Mailardet's Automation. Understanding Simple Machines: Levers.
  URL: http://www.fi.edu/pieces/knox/automation/lever.htm.
  Accessed: April 5, 2003.

Miller, F. 1967. *College Physics, Second Edition*. Harcourt, Brace & World,
  Inc.: New York, NY.

Mustang Survival. FAQ's.
  URL: http://www.mustangsurvival.com/education/ faq.asp.
  Accessed: March 12, 2003.

NASA. Candle Lab.
  URL: http://nasaexplores.com/lessons/01-064/9-12_1-t.html.
  Accessed: March 3, 2003.

Orienteering Definition.
  URL: http://www2.aos.princeton.edu/rdslater/orienteering/
    definitions/orienteering.html.
  Accessed: February 2, 2003.

Ortleb, E.P., and R. Cadice 1991. *Electricity and Magnetism*. Millikin
  Publishing Co.: St. Louis, MO.

Ortleb, E.P., and R. Cadice 1993. *Physical and Chemical Changes*. Millikin
  Publishing Co.: St. Louis, MO.

Ortleb, E.P., and R. Cadice. 1993. *Machines & Work*. Milliken Publishing
  Co.: St. Louis, MO.

Photonet. Colour Vision 1.
  URL: http://www.photo.net/photo/edscott/vis00010.htm.
  Accessed: March 12, 2002.

Purves, W.K., Orians, G.H., and Heller, H.C. 1992. *Life: The Science of
  Biology*. Sinauer Assoc. Inc.: Sunderland, MA.

Rae-Chute, M. Spotted Owl Extinction Plan?
  URL: http://www.bcen.bc.ca/bcerart/Vol8/spottedo.htm.
  Accessed: April 5, 2003.

Rainbow. Rainbow Features.
URL: http://hyperphysics.phy-astr.gsu.edu/hbase/atmos/
rbowfeat.html.
Accessed: March 30, 2003.

Rainbow Physics. Why Are There Rainbows?
URL: http://www.webnexus.com/users/billv/rainbow.
Accessed: March 23, 2003.

Rainbows.
URL: http://www.yorku.ca/eye/rainbow.htm.
Accessed: March 23, 2003.

Rainforest Action Network. 2001. Rainforest Information: Biodiversity.
URL: http://www.rainforestweb.org/Rainforest_Information/
Biodiversity/?state=more.
Accessed: February 2, 2003.

Science Year S.C.I.S.P.Y Top Secret Activity Dossier for
Junior Intelligence Agents.
URL: http://www.scienceyear.com/outthere/parents/SpyBox.pdf.
Accessed: Feburary 23, 2003.

Speed of Sound in Air.
URL: http://adelie.harva5d.edu/ed/Activities/Speed_of_sound.htm.
Accessed: April 3, 2003.

Spike's Science Projects. Home Science Liquids.
URL: http://spikesworld.spike-jamie.com/science/liquids_website/
c122%2036%20watching%20substances%20dissolve.html.
Accessed: April 13, 2003.

Stockley, C., Oxlade, C., Wertheim, J., Rogers, K. 1999. *The Usborne
Illustrated Dictionary of Science*. Usborne Publishing Ltd: London,
England.

Toole, B. Ada: Enchantress of Numbers, Ada Lovelace Biography.
URL: http://www.well.com/user/adatoole/bio.htm.
Accessed: March 30, 2003.

Townsend, A. 1999. The Northern Spotted Owl.
  URL: http://www.personal.psu.edu/users/a/j/ajt155/
    northernspottedowl.html.
  Accessed: April 5, 2003.

UF (*University of Florida News*). February 26, 2003. Obese people
  experience delay in feeling full, UF researchers find.
  URL: http://www.napa.ufl.edu/2003news/obesefullness.htm.
  Accessed: June 22, 2003

USA Today. Weather Basics: Rain, Sun Spawn Nature's Artwork.
  URL: http://www.usatoday.com/weather/tg/wrainbow/wrainbow.htm.
  Accessed: March 23, 2003.

Utah State University. Archimedes of Syracuse: The Father of Buoyancy.
  URL: http://www.engineering.usu.edu/jrestate/workship/buoyancy.htm.
  Accessed: January 1, 2003.

Visible Radiation. Lighting.
  URL: http://site.tekotago.ac.nz/staff/lgodman/drawing/info/Tech/
    Lighting/Lightinga.html.
  Accessed: March 23, 2003.

Waddington, G. 2000. "How the World Was Wired." *YES MAG* 17, Spring:
  14–21.

Warnock, A. 1990. Sound Transmission through Concrete Block Walls.
  URL: http://irc.nrc-cnrc.gc.ca/practice/noi1_E.html.
  Accessed: April 5, 2003.

What Is the Colour Spectrum?
  URL: http://www.colourware.co.uk/cpfaq/q1-1.htm.
  Accessed: March 23, 2003.

About the Author

Tanya Lloyd Kyi hails from Creston, BC. She found a practical use for science early on, when she created a homemade burglar alarm out of an electronics kit in order to keep her sister out of her bedroom. A steady diet of adventure stories such as *The Secret Seven* and *Famous Five* series instilled in her a desire to create strong, smart female characters when she became a writer.

She left Creston after high school to study at the University of Victoria. Since then, she has become a full-time writer and book designer. She wrote *Canadian Girls Who Rocked the World*, *Truth*, and a number of North American travel titles.

When she's not writing or designing, Tanya can be found playing Ultimate, whatever the weather. Failing that, you might find her biking or training for a half-marathon. She continues to investigate the mysteries of everyday science such as the chemical reaction caused by hairspray hitting contact lenses and the impact of chocolate on the brain. She lives in Vancouver, BC.

SCIENCE SQUAD
ADVENTURE SERIES
#1

SUMMER
OF SUSPENSE

Kristin Butcher

Meet the Science Squad: Gina, Sue and Nicole. They have an uncanny knack for getting in trouble and using science to get out of it.

When a series of thefts occurs at a crowded aquarium, the girls use their skills to solve the mystery. Why was the old man arguing with the guards? Was the blind man bumping into people on purpose?

Later, when a fire destroys the work of an inventor, they try to discover who started the suspicious blaze. But why doesn't the woman who lost everything want to find out what really happened?

As the Science Squad sifts through the clues in each story, readers can follow along with sidebars containing explanations of science concepts as well as interesting experiments. It's an interactive and engaging science adventure.

ISBN 1-55285-362-4